"WHAT HAPPENS FROM HERE?"

Ty's change in mood threw her off balance. "I . . . don't know what you mean," Leigh said.

He lifted his hands and sat back slightly on the bed. "You decide and tell me what to do. If you say go—I go."

She opened her mouth but before she could speak he warned her, "But just remember, it had better be what you really want."

"I've already told you I want you to leave—"

"You didn't mean it."

"I told you to go."

"Tell me again." The words were clipped, cool. "And remember, if you do—I won't be back. My system can only stand so much of your brand of stop-and-go loving, Leigh."

A CANDLELIGHT ECSTASY ROMANCE ®

138 WHITE SAND, WILD SEA, *Diana Blayne*
139 RIVER ENCHANTMENT, *Emma Bennett*
140 PORTRAIT OF MY LOVE, *Emily Elliott*
141 LOVING EXILE, *Eleanor Woods*
142 KINDLE THE FIRES, *Tate McKenna*
143 PASSIONATE APPEAL, *Elise Randolph*
144 SURRENDER TO THE NIGHT, *Shirley Hart*
145 CACTUS ROSE, *Margaret Dobson*
146 PASSION AND ILLUSION, *Bonnie Drake*
147 LOVE'S UNVEILING, *Samantha Scott*
148 MOONLIGHT RAPTURE, *Prudence Martin*
149 WITH EVERY LOVING TOUCH, *Nell Kincaid*
150 ONE OF A KIND, *Jo Calloway*
151 PRIME TIME, *Rachel Ryan*
152 AUTUMN FIRES, *Jackie Black*
153 ON WINGS OF MAGIC, *Kay Hooper*
154 A SEASON FOR LOVE, *Heather Graham*
155 LOVING ADVERSARIES, *Eileen Bryan*
156 KISS THE TEARS AWAY, *Anna Hudson*
157 WILDFIRE, *Cathie Linz*
158 DESIRE AND CONQUER, *Diane Dunaway*
159 A FLIGHT OF SPLENDOR, *Joellyn Carroll*
160 FOOL'S PARADISE, *Linda Vail*
161 A DANGEROUS HAVEN, *Shirley Hart*
162 VIDEO VIXEN, *Elaine Raco Chase*
163 BRIAN'S CAPTIVE, *Alexis Hill Jordan*
164 ILLUSIVE LOVER, *Jo Calloway*
165 A PASSIONATE VENTURE, *Julia Howard*
166 NO PROMISE GIVEN, *Donna Kimel Vitek*
167 BENEATH THE WILLOW TREE, *Emma Bennett*
168 CHAMPAGNE FLIGHT, *Prudence Martin*
169 INTERLUDE OF LOVE, *Beverly Sommers*
170 PROMISES IN THE NIGHT, *Jackie Black*
171 HOLD LOVE TIGHTLY, *Megan Lane*
172 ENDURING LOVE, *Tate McKenna*
173 RESTLESS WIND, *Margaret Dobson*
174 TEMPESTUOUS CHALLENGE, *Eleanor Woods*
175 TENDER TORMENT, *Harper McBride*
176 PASSIONATE DECEIVER, *Barbara Andrews*
177 QUIET WALKS THE TIGER, *Heather Graham*

A NIGHT TO REMEMBER

Shirley Hart

A CANDLELIGHT ECSTASY ROMANCE ®

Published by
Dell Publishing Co., Inc.
1 Dag Hammarskjold Plaza
New York, New York 10017

Copyright © 1983 by Shirley Larson

All rights reserved. No part of this book may be
reproduced or transmitted in any form or by any
means, electronic or mechanical, including photocopying,
recording or by any information storage
and retrieval system, without the written permission
of the Publisher, except where permitted by law.

Dell ® TM 681510, Dell Publishing Co., Inc.
Candlelight Ecstasy Romance®, 1,203,540, is a registered
trademark of Dell Publishing Co., Inc.,
New York, New York.

ISBN: 0-440-16320-X

Printed in the United States of America
First printing—October 1983

To Our Readers:

We have been delighted with your enthusiastic response to Candlelight Ecstasy Romances®, and we thank you for the interest you have shown in this exciting series.

In the upcoming months we will continue to present the distinctive sensuous love stories you have come to expect only from Ecstasy. We look forward to bringing you many more books from your favorite authors and also the very finest work from new authors of contemporary romantic fiction.

As always, we are striving to present the unique, absorbing love stories that you enjoy most—books that are more than ordinary romance.

Your suggestions and comments are always welcome. Please write to us at the address below.

> Sincerely,
>
> The Editors
> Candlelight Romances
> 1 Dag Hammarskjold Plaza
> New York, New York 10017

CHAPTER ONE

His lean face dark with impatience, Ty Rundell drove with a careless hand, his fingertips just touching the steering wheel of the car. The setting sun careened off his sunglasses, glistened in the coal-black strands of his hair, highlighted the bones and dark teak color of his cheeks. Below those cheeks, his jaw was taut, hard-edged. Tension had him strung tight as a bowstring. He was getting very close.

From the other side of the car Deke Slayton gave him a sidelong glance and pressed his Western boots against the floor of the car in a vain effort to relieve his cramped thigh muscles. In contrast to Ty's expensive leather car coat and soft wool pants, Deke's jeans and matching denim jacket were a soft, well-worn shade of blue.

Ty slanted a black eyebrow upward, and a slight smile curved his well-shaped lips. "Think you can stand it another fifteen miles?"

"I don't have much choice," Deke said wryly, "unless we pass a place with some good-looking horseflesh and I get out and steal the critter."

"They'll hang you for the horse thief you are," Ty drawled.

Deke smiled, unconcerned. "Better than being cooped up in this little box on wheels."

"I told you to stay home this trip," Ty said easily, unperturbed.

"Yeah." Deke spun the word out.

"It's probably a wild-goose chase." Ty hesitated, scowled. "Maybe her stepfather gave us the wrong information. She might not even be here." He thought about that, his black brows drawn together, the slashing lines beside his mouth deepening. The beauty of the New York State countryside, rampant with the colors of Indian summer October, flaming red and burnished gold and bright orange, was lost on him. The hills that rose to the sky on each side of the road might have been the Los Angeles Freeway for all the attention he paid them.

"But if she is, it'll sure be worth the trip to see her." Ty frowned, turned the wheel to guide the small car around a sharp curve. "Maybe not."

Deke made a sound in the depth of his throat. "Claire Foster's daughter? She ought to be a knockout."

"There's no 'ought' when it comes to heredity. Nature has tricks up her sleeve we haven't even begun to fathom."

"Are you saying you think she won't be good-looking?"

Ty moved his shoulders under the oxblood-colored leather. "I'm not saying anything of the kind. I'm just trying to approach this project with an open mind. Preconceived ideas or personal prejudices can send you down the wrong track."

"Too bad we couldn't get any recent pictures to look at. In most of the ones we saw, she was a little girl or a too-thin teenager with a long face. She still didn't look plain, though. The bone structure was there." Deke slanted him a look and took a small tobacco pouch out of his pocket. With deft, practiced movements he rolled a cigarette, and when he finished, he lit it with a wooden match, drew heavily, and tossed the match in the ashtray, a satisfied look smoothing the lines in his face. "Can't remember you being so fussy"—a stream of blue smoke came into the air—"about preconceived ideas on your last movie."

The sweet tobacco smell of Deke's cigarette drifted to

Ty's nose. He had quit smoking over three years ago, but every once in a while Deke's cigarettes made him feel the old need. Irritated, he said shortly, "That was different. I knew where I was going on that one, right from the start."

Deke looked at the end of his cigarette reflectively. 'And you don't this time?"

"No." The admission was almost a growl.

Deke tapped his cigarette against the ashtray and half turned to face him. Ty had been snappish since they'd gone through those old pictures of Claire Foster and her daughter a week ago. "You're too close to this side of the road," he grumbled. "This isn't Watkins Glen, you know. There's a ravine down there."

Ty smiled. "Nervous?"

The road dipped sharply and then climbed up again. Deke was silent, but his disapproval lingered in the car like the smoke of his cigarette.

"Afraid I've lost my touch?" Ty taunted lazily.

"If God meant men to race in cars, He wouldn't have given them legs," Deke muttered. "Good God. What's that?"

"It looks like a yellow banner telling us it's downhill all the way for a mile and a quarter."

Deke had been a Hollywood stunt man for years, one of the best, doing stunts that other men refused to do, falls from horses or high buildings. He was as brave as any man Ty knew, but he had this peculiar phobia about cars. He had told Ty once that he'd had a dream, and in the dream he'd been killed in a car accident. Ty had laughed and told him he was crazy.

The downward pull of gravity increased their speed. Ty controlled the car easily, turning around a curve. He tapped the brakes once experimentally, toyed with the idea of shifting into a lower gear, and decided against it.

"Don't get your hopes up," Ty said lazily, more to divert Deke from the swiftly moving scenery outside their window than anything else. "Claire's daughter is a schoolteacher. She probably wears black health shoes and her hair in a bun." He put his foot on the brake, his mouth curved in a smile—until he heard that sudden little ping—and his foot slapped the floorboard. The smile vanished. He sat up and gripped the wheel, moving his foot up and down, easily at first, then quicker, harder, with more determination. The brake pedal sank to the floor—and the car careened on.

His worst fears confirmed, the blood drained away from his face. He rammed his foot down on the clutch and shifted to third, praying the gears would mesh. They did. The car jerked, slowing.

Deke was thrown forward into his seat belt. "What the hell are you trying to do, get us killed?" He scowled and turned to Ty. "This isn't the Grand Prix—"

"Just hang on," he gritted. His hands gripped the wheel, knuckles white with the strength and energy he was using to guide the car. He could drive out of it as long as there were no unsuspecting pedestrians at the bottom of the hill. The thought made perspiration bead on his brow, drip down his back under his cotton shirt.

Deke growled, "We're going too fast. What the hell is wrong?"

"No brakes," he said tersely. When Deke half roused as if he were going to jump out, Ty grated, "Don't be a fool. Sit still. Our best bet is to ride this out. I've still got the emergency." He pulled back on the lever, but their speed barely slackened.

"That's great," Deke muttered, his voice heavy with irony. "Really brought us up short. Listen, man, we've got to do something—"

The road followed another sharp curve, and he could hear the grind of the motor as it worked to stay in the lower gear. "Just hang on."

They flew through a village, a wide place in the road

called Webster's Crossing. He caught a brief glimpse of a woman's face, her features a mixture of horror and dread. They were obviously not the first car to go flying past her down that hill.

Another swoop of the car, another curve brought them to the last final sharp drop. He'd given up using the emergency, thinking he'd save it for use toward the end. He could see Springwater now, drowsy in the sun, unaware of the juggernaut bearing toward it. He cursed, wondering why this should be happening to him. He'd had the car inspected a couple of months ago, and the brakes had been fine then.

He gripped the wheel tighter and steeled himself for the final plummet down the hill. Out of the corner of his eye, he caught a glimpse of Deke's white face. He cursed again and wondered if Deke's dream would come true for both of them. Then he saw it, the caution light strung over the street and the crossroad that intersected the road he was on. Heading down the crossroad on a direct collision course with him was a small blue car. Desperate, he flattened his palm against the horn. It gave out a bleep, a small, pathetic sound, but it was all he had, and he kept it going.

Gears grinding, the car flew into the town. He had a vague impression of white buildings, the glass front of an antique shop. But ahead of him the road continued straight and—thank God—angled upward. Out of the corner of his eye, he saw blue metal coming toward him. He slammed the clutch to the floor, shifted into a higher gear, and accelerated past the intersection at an even faster rate of speed. They slid by the other car with inches to spare and were running up the steep side of another hill. Already feeling the loss of speed on the incline, he rammed the clutch in again and shifted to a lower gear. The pull of gravity working with the motor made the car lose speed. Ty yanked back on the emergency brake. The car stopped.

He turned off the motor and slumped in his seat, too shaken to move. Deke sat beside him, and in the little car he could hear the rasp of Deke's breathing. He turned to look at him. The older man was white around the mouth, his eyes blank. "You all right?"

Deke's drawl was forced. "Yeah—thanks to you."

Running feet pounded against the asphalt, and the door on Ty's side flew open. A young woman bent down to peer at him, and all he could think of was that she had the most gorgeous mane of honey-blond hair he had ever seen. From under a ridiculous bowler hat, the spun gold tresses swung forward over her shoulder and trapped the sun in a thousand little shimmering lights.

"Are you all right?" Her voice was slightly husky, like the rasp of velvet on velvet.

He didn't think he was. He thought he must be seeing things. She was a sparkling portrait of color and contrast, vivid iridescent gray eyes set in an ivory skin, gleaming brown lashes, a wide, generous, and utterly lovely mouth moistened with a soft rose gloss.

His eyes wandered lower, and then he knew this vision didn't really exist. The accident was making him hallucinate. Here, in this tiny upstate town, he had conjured up an unbelievable woman—a woman dressed to ride to the hounds. She wore the traditional English hunting regalia, black velvet jacket, a crisp white ruffled shirt, tight-fitting fawn-colored pants that hugged her shapely legs and were tucked into the tops of shiny black boots. The only out-of-place thing about her was the dust on the gloved hand she extended toward him.

"I've put blocks behind the car. You won't roll back. You're safe now. Can you get out? What about your friend?"

He nodded, tore his eyes away from her to look at Deke. Deke sat with his head back, his eyes closed. The color had not come back to his face. Ty shook his head and turned to the woman again to grasp her gloved hand. It was surprisingly firm and strong, the gloved fingers wrapping around his with a tensile grip that startled him.

"Watch your knees," she warned. "You may be a little unsteady. Sometimes the shock is delayed."

Ty was rapidly regaining his ability to think. Briefly, he considered lurching against that trim body with its womanly curves accented in men's garb, but a sudden sharp distaste filled him at the idea. Those clear gray eyes with their look of concern deserved better from him. She was right about one thing, though. His legs were decidedly unsteady.

He gripped her hand and steadied himself by grasping the roof of the car with the other. He shot her a quick glance, expecting a mocking smile, but her face still held nothing but concern. He said, "Thanks for the warning. I didn't—expect to feel so—blitzed."

"Most people don't," she said calmly.

"Does this happen often?" He didn't release his hold on her hand.

"Once a year," she said, shrugging, lifting a shoulder under the black velvet.

"Once a year?" He was astounded. "Why in God's name isn't something done?"

"What do you suggest?" she asked dryly. "Rebuilding the entire town on the top of the hill? There *are* signs warning trucks to take other routes. That's about all that can be done. The townspeople try to keep alert." She shot him a bland look and pulled her hand free from his grasp, leaving him feeling suddenly chilled and alone. "If people took better care of their cars, we wouldn't need to worry."

A dark tide of color rose under his cheekbones. "I had the brakes checked a couple of months ago."

She shrugged, obviously unwilling to pursue the matter. Her eyes flickered over him, and he caught that brief flare of feminine interest. Then, something happened. The warmth, the sexual appraisal was damped down sharply, and long carmel-colored eyelashes blocked her eyes from his view. She liked his looks—but for some reason she didn't want him to know it. She had withdrawn emotionally, and now she distanced herself physically as well, turning away from him to look up the hill. The sun had dropped lower, and there was a decided chill in the air. "Life is full of things we'd like to change and—can't." There was something in her voice, a husky catch that made him think she wasn't talking about the hill.

He watched the fading light play over her face and felt a blazing elation take fire in him just from looking at her. God, what would happen if he ever touched that cool ivory skin? He'd go up in smoke. "I'd like to thank you, Miss—"

She turned toward him, and every scrap of warmth and concern left her face. Her eyes were icy, chilling the air around him. She had caught the vibration of his interest, and she didn't like it.

"There's no need to thank me." She pivoted sharply, her boot making a rasping sound on the rough surface of the road. She was going to walk out of his life, and he didn't even know who she was. Panicked, he said roughly, "I'll need a place to stay for the night. Any suggestions?"

"There are no motels." The words were crisp. "Try Mrs. Tyler. She runs a boardinghouse just down the street—"

A man's voice called, "Leigh! Darling, are you all right? Helen told me you were nearly hit—"

She had taken a step away from him, but at the sound of that name, Ty fought back the feeling of being punched in the solar plexus and covered the ground between them with two quick movements of his long legs. His hand reached out, grasped the velvet-clad arm. "Were you in that blue car? My God, I nearly annihilated you!"

She gave his hard, angry face a cool look and shook her

arm, clearly inviting him to release his hold on her. He didn't. She said, "I heard your horn and slammed on the brakes. You had the good sense to increase your speed. Not many men would have been thinking as clearly."

He wasn't thinking clearly at the moment. Right now, his thoughts were a muddle. That cool, unwillingly given bit of praise stirred his senses, and that wasn't the only thing about her that disturbed him. Her perfume drifted to his nose, and the closeness of that enticing curve of breast to his fingers invited him to brush his knuckles over the rounded firmness of her. Bluntly, not thinking, only wanting her confirmation, he said, "You're Leigh Carlow."

He saw the emotions flash in her eyes in rapid succession, the disbelief, the withdrawal, the anger—and finally, the contempt. She made a sound in her throat and pulled at her arm just as the man who had called ran panting up the hill toward them and came within hearing distance, but Ty held her, his fingers slipping down to clamp around the fine bones of her wrist.

Leigh was equally aware of the other man's approach. Ty felt her tremble with anger under his hand, but she had herself in superb control and her voice stayed on that same low, beautifully husky but feminine pitch. "My stepfather warned me you were coming." She took a breath, as if she had been running. "If you write one word about me, I'll sue you for defamation of character and libel, and anything else that comes to mind. Do I make myself clear?"

"As crystal, Miss Carlow." He held her arm for a moment longer, watching temper turn her eyes to molten silver. He wondered what color those eyes were when she was making love. . . . He dropped her arm and gave her a mocking bow of his dark head. They were behind the car now, and he saw how she had propped cement blocks behind each wheel. Where had she got them from? How had she carried them there so quickly? "Thank you for the cement blocks. I'm sure I'll be seeing you again soon—"

Her mouth twisted. "That's not possible, Mr. Writer-Producer, whoever you are. As soon as you get your car fixed, you'd better leave Springwater."

His mouth lifted in a mocking smile. "Is that a threat?"

She gave a short, unamused laugh. "It's a simple fact. There's no reason for you to stay."

Before he could reply, the man who had called moments ago huffed up beside them. He was dressed in a hunting outfit, too, but his hair was a silver gray, and his body thick with middle age, and he looked more incongruent than ever standing beside the tall, slim woman who wore the same clothes with such style and grace. The pair of half glasses perched on his nose underlined the difference in their ages. He peered over these at Leigh. "Darling, are you all right?"

"I'm fine, Hunt." She extended her hand to him as she had to Ty, and Hunt took it with a proprietorial air. Ty felt a surge of cold rage. My God, the man was old enough to be her father.

He gave Ty a curious look, and Ty seized on the man's interest to say, "Leigh."

She turned back, her eyes glacial. "What do you want?"

There was a question. "Where am I going to find this—Mrs. Tyler?"

Her companion gave her a half-shocked, half-amused look. "Darling, you're not fobbing him off on Lelia Tyler, are you? The place you stay is much nicer. And Viola Hendricks's second-floor apartment is vacant; you told me that yourself, just the other day."

Leigh Carlow's face was pale with anger, but she said in a careful, controlled tone, "Mrs. Tyler is close."

Hunt turned to Ty. "Don't listen to her," he said expansively. "Viola Hendricks has a nice old house that sits beside the creek, and she's an immaculate housekeeper.

Just go up this road and turn where the sign says Springwater Creek Public Fishing. It's a brick house with a glassed-in front porch and green shutters. Fourth on your right. Sign in front says Rooms for Rent. You can't miss it."

He looked at Leigh Carlow's pale face, saw the tightening of that attractive mouth. "Thank you, Mr.—"

"Beatty, Hunt Beatty." The man released Leigh's hand and offered his to Ty. "Ty Rundell," Ty said softly, his eyes flickering over them both, watching the darkening of her pupils at the sound of his name.

"You know Leigh."

"We were just—introducing ourselves"—his smile played over her cool face—"when you arrived. I was expressing my gratitude to Miss Carlow for her help."

Hunt Beatty threw a careless arm over Leigh's shoulder, and Ty felt an overwhelming urge to break it for him. "Leigh's a very cool-headed woman. Handy to have around."

"I should imagine," Ty drawled, watching with interest at the way the tone of his voice made the pupils of her eyes flare and her cheeks pulse with hot color.

"My God." The groaned words came from inside the car. "What hit me?"

Deke Slayton appeared at the edge of the car, holding his head. "I feel as if I've been on a twelve-day drunk."

He staggered forward, then leaned back against the car, propping himself against it. Almost at once, Leigh was beside him, supporting him, a cool hand on his head. "You must have fainted."

Deke groaned and lifted his head to look first at her and then at Ty. "For God's sake, don't tell anyone back at the lot this happened. I feel as if I've been hit by a ten-ton truck."

"Shock," Leigh said succinctly. "Some people take things harder than others." She gave Ty an icy look.

19

"You'll get over it." She turned away. "Hunt, we'll be late for the party."

Hunt Beatty's full cheeks filled with color. "It hardly seems in good taste to go away and just—leave them like this." He gave Ty a quick, guilty look. Ty went to Deke and stepped next to him, throwing one of Deke's arms over his shoulder, facing the other couple, surreptitiously giving Deke a light kidney punch that made him sag against Ty in surprise. "He's all right," Ty said, gripping Deke's shoulder in warning, keeping his voice expressionless, his face stoic in the best piece of acting he'd done in a long time. "He'll be able to walk—eventually."

Hunt Beatty took the bait. "Leigh, they've had a bad scare. We can run them up to Viola's in your car; it would only take a minute."

Ty gave her full marks for poise. She didn't betray a thing; not a movement of her mouth or eyes gave her away. "Yes, of course." Without another word, she pivoted and strode down the hill ahead of them, leaving Hunt to help Ty half carry a dazed Deke down the incline.

Hunt insisted they wait until Ty brought their luggage. Ty propped Deke against Leigh's blue car, made the return trip, collected their bags, and locked the crippled car.

Seated in the backseat of Leigh's blue Omni with Deke, Ty heard her say something to Hunt Beatty, but that low tone of hers didn't carry, and he didn't catch her words. Beside him, Deke muttered, "What the hell is going on? Why the rabbit punch?"

"Just keep quiet and look sick," Ty ordered in a low undertone.

"No problem." Deke groaned and closed his eyes.

Viola Hendricks reminded Ty of a small, friendly snapping turtle with her hunched shoulders and bright dark eyes. Her snow-white hair was styled in tight little ringlets that seemed to spring up from her head instead of grow out of it.

"You can have the one on the second floor," she said after a quick cursory glance over Ty's jacket and shoes. He had no doubt she could have told him the price of both articles of clothing within five dollars. "Just got the place cleaned today."

Hunt Beatty had insisted on helping them carry their luggage in, but now, probably because of that low-voiced remark of Leigh's, he seemed anxious to leave them. Leigh had remained in the car, with the motor running for a quick getaway, Ty thought, his mouth twisting in unconscious reaction.

Mrs. Hendricks gave him a quick, stabbing look. "Can you climb the stairs?"

"Yeah," he said quickly, knowing that she had reacted to his grimace brought on by the thought of Leigh's dislike for him. Country people watched you too damn closely. They didn't just let their eyes drift over you and quickly look away like people in the city did. He had to remember that. He picked up his bag and followed Deke up the stairs.

By eleven o'clock Leigh was ready to leave the gym with its mass of churning teenage life and go home. Kevin Clark had spilled his punch on Jennifer Redfern's antebellum dress, sending her weeping into the ladies' room. By the time Leigh managed to sponge off the red stain and return Jennifer to a red-faced Kevin, Leigh was convinced that the music would, in another instant, render her completely deaf.

Melting pools of ice cream and cake on flimsy paper plates sat around on the floor under the folding chairs. For something to do, she began to pick them up. Her stomach had been strangely queasy this evening. She hadn't been able to finish the portion that Hunt had brought her an hour before. Maybe it had been the close call she'd had. . . . Her eyes darkened as she remembered. Resolutely, she thrust the thought of the lean man with his hard, cynically attractive face from her thoughts. She was losing her mind. Had she really believed having a costume party to encourage her students to research different people in history and their clothes a good idea? She ought to have her head looked at. What had seemed like a marvelous idea in September had become an October nightmare.

She sighed and walked across the hall to dump her unsightly collection of soupy paper plates into a plastic barrel. She turned back and stood in the doorway, watching. To be fair, some of her students had done a marvelous job of re-creating period pieces of clothing. A pioneer woman danced with a Greek-togaed senator, who kept losing his sheet off one shoulder; a Scarlett O'Hara danced with a Rhett Butler, who had found a fake mustache from somewhere; and an Indian brave in authentic war paint was doing the Watusi with Cleopatra. There was even a young couple from Star Trek wearing tights, their tunics marked with the insignia of the Star Fleet.

"Swell dance, Miss Carlow." Kevin Clark, determined to reinstate himself in her good graces after his earlier faux pas, gyrated around to yell at her above the din. A mollified Jennifer danced in front of him in an approximation of the awkward steps he executed.

She nodded and smiled, something she seemed to have done so often this evening her mouth was in danger of cracking.

Hunt was out on the floor, dancing. Max, the art teacher, who was also her stepfather's cousin, had a generous amount of Dean's patience. Max regarded chaperoning student events as a pleasure rather than a pain and needed his head looked at as much as she did. He sauntered over to her, a cup of punch in his hand.

"He's in his glory," he said, nodding out toward Hunt and then turning, smiling at her. He was almost shouting.

"He can handle things for a while. Come outside and catch some silence with me."

She nodded ruefully and shouted back, "What a great idea."

Outside, the quiet was sudden, soothing, making her feel as if she'd been pushing against something for hours and it had given way. The air was cool, and the black velvet jacket that had been far too heavy for the heated air inside was just right for the crispness of the night air.

They wandered down the sidewalk, the school a dark flat shadow behind them, and Leigh knew Max was relishing the silence as much as she was. A breeze tossed a cloud over the almost-full moon, and the golden maple at the end of the walk rustled silkily.

Max turned slightly to look at her. "Hunt tells me you had a close call today."

A flicker of annoyance touched her. "It was nothing, really—"

"I wouldn't call getting almost killed 'nothing.' Some chap from California, Hunt said."

Leigh nodded, her face averted, the shadow of a moving leaf tracing patterns over her cheek.

"Was he somebody who knew your mother?"

She shook her head. "Dean sent him here." The puzzled hurt was there in her voice for Max to hear.

"That's strange. Doesn't sound like something Dean would do. He must have had a reason. . . ."

"He—called me to warn me the man was coming."

Max frowned with concern. "If you need any help, Leigh, you know where I am."

"I won't need any help," she shot back. "I can take care of myself."

"Dean would never forgive me if—"

"At the age of twenty-seven I think I'm finally able to manage my own life, Max."

He shrugged. "It isn't something that comes automatically with age. Some people never learn the trick."

"Please, just don't tell this—producer anything if he comes around to you, will you?"

Max gave her a wry look. "As if I would."

Two hours later, she chided herself for having to reassure herself of Max's reticence, but her encounter with Ty Rundell had thrown her, and she was still distracted as she worked with Hunt and Max and two other women teachers in the suddenly quiet schoolhouse to clean up the debris of the party. It was after twelve o'clock when the soggy paper plates had all been disposed of and the punch bowl washed and the floor swept, and when she walked out into the cool night again, she felt drained. Hunt seemed not to notice her silence as he walked her to her car.

But he must have noticed something, for as he stood beside the car with her, he leaned forward, gave her a light peck on the forehead, and said, "Go on home, darling. It's a beautiful night. I'll walk."

"No, Hunt, I can take you—"

"Nonsense. It's all of four blocks. I need the exercise to cool down."

She made another weak protest which he answered with an adamant refusal. With a warm feeling for his understanding, she got into the car alone, knowing that conversation or coffee with Hunt in her apartment would have been impossible to tolerate.

CHAPTER TWO

She climbed the stairs, and when she reached the first landing and saw the sliver of light under the door, she remembered that she was no longer alone on the upper two stories of Viola's house. The rooms below her loft were occupied. Did sound carry between the floors? She had never worried about that before, but now she did, and it seemed like too much, an added thorn to dig into her flesh beside the deeper ones that first the stranger and then Max had so unwittingly slid under her skin.

Her foot came down on the second to the last step from the top, and the groan of creaking wood echoed through the house like a gunshot, reverberating against the plastered walls and the oak woodwork. She chided herself for not remembering to step over it. If anyone was awake in that second-floor apartment, they would surely know that she was on her way up to hers. Still faintly annoyed at her absentmindedness, she took out her key and unlocked her door.

She slipped out of the black jacket with a sense of being set free, unbuttoned the shirt, stripped off the boots and trousers, and hung the clothes neatly on the hanger. The entire outfit would have to go back to the city tomorrow. Hunt had said he would return it for her along with his. She was glad it would be gone from her sight. She wouldn't have to look at it and remember that dark, cynical face that had gazed up at her from the car with its slightly dazed expression because of the clothes she wore. . . .

She padded into the bathroom in bare feet, stripped out of her underthings, poked her hair under a yellow, flower-sprigged cap, and got into the shower. She had felt sorry for him. What a fool she was.

You'd be better off to sympathize with a panther.

He was a predator on the prowl, and he was hoping to snare her in his net and put her on public display. *Look at the peculiar specimen I've bagged, ladies and gentlemen, the daughter of the sultry sex symbol Claire Foster.*

She turned her face up into the spray, letting the water pour over her skin. If only water had the magic power to take away her memories.

The picture of Dean flashed into her mind, tall, solid, his red and black lumberman's plaid jacket stretched across wide shoulders. *Would you have the one good thing in your life washed away with all the bad? Would you forget the one man your mother married who was worth a damn?*

She turned off the water, stepped out of the shower. What kind of alchemy had this—Ty Rundell—used on Dean to get him to divulge her whereabouts? Through the years, her stepfather had been the one man she could trust, the one man who had all her love. He had sent others away in droves. He was utterly incorruptible—he loved only his cabin in the Adirondacks and his life in the wilderness . . . and Leigh. Fame, money, meant nothing to him. Dean was cool, logical, observant, and far more intelligent than most people recognized on the first meeting. It hit her then, as she swathed herself in the terry cloth robe, that Dean had to have some reason for putting this man on a direct route to her door. What could it have been?

The soft knock came just as she emerged from the bathroom. Her heart kicked up, accelerated. She considered not answering, but that would be childish—and cowardly. No man was going to reduce her to being afraid to answer her own door. She snatched the shower cap from her head, letting her hair spill over her shoulders, and pulled the terry cloth belt tighter around her middle before she opened the door.

He was there dressed in jeans and a T-shirt, his feet bare. "I'm sorry to bother you," Ty Rundell said, and for some reason she believed him. "Deke woke up with this killer of a headache about twenty minutes ago, and neither of us has anything. Do you happen to have—"

"I'll get you something." She went back into the bathroom and returned with a bottle of white tablets. She held them out, and he took them, his fingers brushing hers briefly at the moment of contact. She fought the urge to stuff her hand into the deep pocket of her terry cloth robe, wished those blue eyes weren't so disturbingly keen, and heard herself saying, "Would you like some ice?"

He hesitated, and then said politely, "Yes, if it isn't too much trouble."

"It's no trouble." Glad to increase the distance between them, she walked across to the kitchenette, which was just a corner of the apartment separated from the rest of the room by a snack bar, fished the small blue ice bag out of the bottom drawer, and, opening the refrigerator, began to fill it with the crushed ice she kept in a tray.

"You seem to be prepared for such—contingencies."

The sound of his voice told her he had come closer. The soft masculine tones crawled over her spine, reminded her of the intimacy of being enclosed with him in her small apartment. She felt rather than heard him take another step, and totally panicked now, she turned around. The slanted ceilings and peaked roof that had seemed airy closed in on her. "I was a Girl Scout," she said, handing him the bag, averting her eyes from the light dusting of dark curling hairs on his chest, the muscular breadth of his shoulders. His panache didn't depend on his expensive clothes; he was just as dangerous to her senses this way, in faded jeans clinging to lean hips and a snug-fitting dark blue T-shirt with a leather belt accenting the hard, flat stomach. He moved toward her to take the bag. She watched the working of his muscles in his shoulders as he extended his arm, and something closed in her throat.

"Deke will appreciate this," he said softly.

She scrambled mentally, trying to remember that it was Deke that had brought Ty Rundell here to her apartment. "I—hope he feels better in the morning."

"He will." Dark lashes flickered down. "Thanks for these. If you're—out tomorrow"—he lifted the bottle, gesturing with it—"I'll leave this with Viola."

"I—yes, fine." She agreed to his arrangements, feeling strangely let down.

With a smooth, lithe movement, he swung away from her. The black velvet of the hunting jacket shone vividly in the bright light, and she could have clocked the moment it caught his eye. She watched his black head move up, his stride slow as he looked at it. At the door, he turned to her. "Did you—catch the fox?"

She met his eyes, instinctively pulling the belt tighter around her waist. "No," she said huskily. "She—got away."

"Too bad." His blue eyes gleamed briefly with some undefinable emotion. "Better luck next time." He strode out the door, leaving her with the feeling of being set adrift on an ocean, its depth unknown—and foreboding.

Two hours later she still had not gone to bed. Seized by a restlessness that would not go away, she hadn't even tried to sleep. She sat in the big, overstuffed armchair, every light in the small sitting room on, a book in her hand that she hadn't looked at since she sat down, gazing out into the darkness through the slanted skylights that faced the north on the creek side of the house, seeing nothing, her mind numb. But when the soft knock came again, every nerve in her body leaped into life.

He was completely dressed this time, wearing the leather jacket over a soft gauzy shirt of a dark gray color, the expensive shoes on his feet. "I've been watching your light, waiting for it to go off," he said, nodding toward the big skylight windows that threw yellow patches of brilliance on the creek and trees below, "and thought since you were up anyway, I'd return these." He held out the bottle of tablets.

She took them. "How is—Deke?"

The well-shaped mouth lifted in a slight smile. "Sleeping like a baby. Your treatment was just what the doctor ordered."

"I'm glad." She let her eyes flicker over him. He was dressed to go out, and she wondered where he was going at this hour of the night.

As if she had spoken her thoughts aloud, he said, "I wasn't so lucky. Can't even close my eyes. I guess that little episode this afternoon bothered me more than I thought it did." He met her gaze steadily. "I keep thinking I could have killed you."

"But you didn't," she said coolly. "We were both—lucky."

"Yes." He spun the word out, giving it an emphasis that made her skin prickle. She braced herself for something, she wasn't sure what, when his shoulders moved dismissively under his jacket and he turned as if he were going to go. But he didn't. Another piercing glance of those blue eyes swept over her. "I often go for a walk about this time of night—just before dawn." A small hesitation. "Would you care to go with me? We do need to—talk."

Those cool blue eyes watched her. His features were shadowed in the half light of the hall, but she could feel him examining her face for the most infinitesimal sign of emotion—and betraying nothing behind that lean, cynical face of his.

She vacillated, weighing the danger. To be wary of him

29

now, at this point, was slightly ridiculous. If he was going to pounce or grab, he would have done it before this. He had had the perfect opportunity two hours ago, and he hadn't done a thing. The attraction must be all one way. He didn't seem interested in her personally. But even though he wasn't interested in her, he had destroyed her peace of mind. Maybe if she spent some time with him, his attraction would diminish. No, that was stupid. If she had a brain in her head, she wouldn't get within a mile of him. "It will take me a minute or two to get dressed," she heard herself tell him, as if her mouth weren't connected to her powers of reasoning.

Before she could see his reaction to her agreement, he turned away. "I'll wait outside," he murmured and walked lightly down the hall, pivoting at the head of the stairs, stretching his long leg past the second riser to avoid that creaking board.

She closed the door, feeling distinctly disturbed. It had taken her two weeks to remember that that step creaked, and she still forgot to avoid it when she was under stress the way she had been tonight. She was crazy to think she could fence with a man that cool, that adaptable.

Ten minutes later, when she stepped out into the chilly night, she was glad she had dressed in warm pants and a quilted ski jacket. She came hesitantly down the walk, wondering where he was. Had he gone without her? A shadow near the trunk of the maple tree moved, and he stepped into the dim light of the moon. She swallowed back a small gasp.

"I'm sorry," he said at once, taking her hand. "I didn't mean to frighten you." He grasped her hand as he might have a child's, but she was plunged into a far deeper level of fear at the warm touch of his fingers on hers. Her breath seemed to cling to her body and refuse to go out again. Ty was a dark shadow beside her, the impetus of his stride moving her along the worn path that led to the creek.

She tried a slight, extremely gentle tug, an almost slipping movement of her fingers that could have been a natural part of her stride, but just as lightly and naturally he tightened his grip, as if it were something he had done a hundred times before on a walk with her.

Fall scented the air, the fragrance of ripening apples and drying corn making a heady brew. Overhead, stars glittered, their brilliance magnified by the cool crispness.

In a low voice he said, "The stars seem close." They walked on for a few steps while he seemed to be thinking. "This little town reminds me of the place where I was born," he said easily. "Except for the hills. Freedom, Wyoming. Do you know of it?"

She shook her head.

"Know why it was called that?"

"No, why?"

"Because it sits on the border between Wyoming and Idaho, and the early Mormons who settled there were searching for the freedom to practice their own religion—and the polygamy they once believed in. When the state of Wyoming made an occasional effort to prosecute, they just moved into Idaho two blocks away. If the Idaho authorities got overzealous, back they went to Wyoming. The law never got its act together—and the Mormons were able to stay in the same town—which must have seemed like a very great freedom to them."

She said, "I thought perhaps you were born in Los Angeles."

"No. I wasn't a show business brat like you. My father works on a ranch. Still does. He thinks I'm crazy—a black mark on the Rundell name."

A faint smile touched her lips. "Is that what he wanted you to do—be a cowboy?"

"Yeah." There was a harshness in the slowly drawled word.

"You didn't—want to be a cowboy?"

"Not working on somebody else's ranch," he grated. "I wasn't cut out to be a hired hand."

She felt a stab of empathy, of understanding so acute that she could almost see him as a young man, chafing under the reins of another man's yoke. They walked along the path that bordered the creek, and the thought of him as a young, ambitious boy in Wyoming with no outlet for his talents dominated her thoughts, but when the shadow of a willow crossed his face and the moon highlighted the dark attraction of his well-shaped head and full, vibrant black hair, she remembered that he was no longer a boy striving to break out of the mold; he was a mature man, a successful writer and producer who moved in the cynical world of show business with a sure knowledge of people and the way to play on their sympathies. She couldn't let herself feel empathy for him. She couldn't feel anything for him. "Is all this—self-examination and delving into your past supposed to encourage me to talk about mine?"

Clamping her hand in a viselike grip, he hauled her around. Even in the dark, she could feel his eyes burning into her. "It wasn't supposed to encourage you to do a damn thing—except listen to a fellow human being talk about the things that keep him awake at night."

In the moonlight, her face was pale, her eyes dark shadows. "I don't feel sorry for you," she shot back at him. "At least you can be proud of your family. They're honest, decent people who work hard for a living. You don't have to be ashamed of them. You don't have to feel your skin crawl every time someone says their name—" Her voice broke.

"Leigh—" He pulled her into his arms, and the sweet, smoky scent of his clothes, the hard contours of his body under the leather made her wild with desperation. She stiffened her arms and threw her head back. "Keep your sympathy."

He tightened his grip and said, "Leigh, just listen to me—"

"No," she cried, panic-stricken. "Let go of me!"

"I can't. Oh, God, I can't." His head shadowed her from the moon, and his mouth came down on hers, hard, demanding, unyielding. His lips welded themselves to hers, and his arms held her in their steel-trap grip, and she was dying . . . dying because she had been catapulted into a bright new world where his lips and hands and body made the aching half of her whole . . . and yet not quite. She wanted more. . . . She fought the dark, rising tide of desire by keeping her lips closed, but he lifted his head and muttered harshly, "Don't kiss me like some teenage kid. Open your mouth, Leigh, let me taste you."

His words were powerful, seductive, and though she fought not to give in, when his mouth hovered over hers, her own softened slowly, tentatively, and at last—allowed him access.

He sensed her surrender at once and swooped, flicking his tongue inside, probing, caressing, thrusting—claiming. An elemental excitement poured through her veins. He was like pure alcohol injected into her bloodstream, dissolving her in effervescence. His intimate kiss was a heady champagne that both satisfied—yet made her thirsty. He submerged her in heat and sensation, his hands finding the zipper of her jacket, running it down, and spreading his fingers over her back to pull her against him more tightly. She wore only a light cotton T-shirt, and the warmth and strength of his hands burned through the thin material, exploring, discovering the place on her back where there should have been a bra clip—and wasn't. His own jacket hung open, and the crush of his body on her breasts and the intimate way he cradled his hips to hers tantalized her with the heady thought that lying under him would be sheer ecstasy. . . .

She fought away from him like a wildcat, clawing, flailing, pushing at him with a strength born of panic and anger. Her sudden resistance startled him, and he thrust her away as if she were a time bomb that had gone off in his hands. "What the hell—"

"I warned you." She panted the words, breathless. "Get out of my life and leave me alone." She whirled around, and a willow twig snapped under her foot. The sound cracked in the silent night.

"Wait a minute." A hard hand on her shoulder caught her, turned her violently around. "What the hell is wrong with you? One minute you're a loving, responsive woman, and the next you're a screaming shrew."

"What's the matter?" She lifted her head and stared at him in the dark, seeing nothing but a tall, angry shape. "Didn't your little game plan work the way you thought it would? Didn't Claire Foster's daughter fall into your arms the way she was supposed to?"

"What are you talking about?"

Pale with anger, her body stiff and tense under the hand that still held her, she said, "I'm talking about your grand plan for seducing Claire Foster's daughter." She threw the words at his dark face. "After all, she ought to be worth it. Her mother was the most celebrated lay in Hollywood—"

His other arm whipped up, and she was caught, both his hands clamped like steel traps on her shoulders. He shook her, just once, very hard. "Stop it! For God's sake, stop it."

Sanity returned. "Let go of me—please, just—let go of me."

He held her for a moment, and she was too exhausted to do anything but wait for his decision. He said, "I'll let you go—on one condition—that we talk about this."

She lifted her chin, pride blazing. "There's nothing to talk about."

"Oh, yes, there is," he shot back, his fingers tightening.

His hands were making her want more, making her want to move into his arms and feel the wild delight of his mouth on hers. . . . "All right. All right. Just take your hands off of me."

He lifted them away. She waited for the release of tension, the relief—but it didn't come. Her body wanted his touch—

"We're going back to your apartment. You can make some coffee." His voice was as crisp and cool as the air that moved over her cheek.

Stung, she retorted, "Don't order me around as if I'm your servant."

Through gritted teeth, he said, "I've told myself I'm not going to strangle you tonight. Don't make me change my mind."

He didn't touch her again, but he stayed behind her as they walked back to the house as if he were a guard with a prisoner. She wasn't his prisoner. She was free—and she had to stay that way.

The brisk walk back through the chilly air had the effect of a cold shower, and by the time they had climbed the stairs and she had unlocked the door, she was reasonably in control.

She turned on the lights quickly, dispelling any illusion of intimacy, and kept her jacket on. She crossed to the kitchenette and took the glass carafe out from under the coffee maker to carry it to the sink and rinse out the residue. She filled the carafe with clean water and was pouring it through when she heard the click of the door that told her he had come inside and closed it.

The small round kitchen table was loaded down with her book bag and the pile of papers that had to be read and corrected before Monday. She pushed them aside and made two places, laying out placemats and cups and saucers.

"Don't fuss."

"I'm not," she said shortly, keeping her back to him, searching for the paper napkins in a middle drawer. She found them—they were pink, left over from the Easter dinner she had served Hunt. She folded them in neat triangles and tucked them under the spoons.

Her voice cool and polite, she asked, "Milk or sugar?"

"Just milk."

The water had dripped through, and she flipped the switch, turning on the warmer. She lifted the carafe and turned to the table to pour the steaming brown liquid into the cups.

Then there was nothing left to do but sit down beside him. He had already seated himself, and he looked completely at home, lounging on the wooden chair with his feet thrust forward, stretched to full length and crossed at the ankles.

She took a sip of coffee, strung up, waiting. He didn't say anything, didn't even seem to be watching her. She might have been in the room by herself. The minutes stretched by endlessly, and if there had been a clock in the room, its ticking would have sounded like thunder. She took another sip of coffee, swallowed it, and could stand it no longer. "I thought you wanted to talk to me."

He glanced up, one dark eyebrow arched in sardonic amusement. "I thought I'd wait until you're ready to listen."

"I'm ready," she said tersely.

He gazed at her. "Leigh, I'd like to be able to tell you that I'm giving up the project." He paused, his blue eyes holding hers.

"But you're not going to," she said, her tone caustic.

"No." The word was drawled in a cool tone. "Your—reaction to me makes it imperative that I—go on."

She shot him a hot, angry look. "What's that supposed to mean?"

He leaned back in the chair, his lashes half concealing

the piercing blueness of his eyes. "Hasn't it ever occurred to you that you aren't the only child of a celebrity in the world? Think about the tragedy of Scott Newman's suicide. There are other people like you, Leigh, people who struggle with a burden so damn heavy they can hardly carry it. I've already talked to some of them. They need help. Maybe if the public was made aware of the problems facing the children of celebrities—"

"And you're going to clarify everything—and make money at the same time."

His lean fingers played over the spoon, clenched it. "Sure, I'll make money. I'm not going to apologize for that. If I didn't, I couldn't go on making pictures."

"That would be a great pity."

The spoon clattered against the table. "You know just where and how hard to hit, don't you?"

She laughed, a short, unamused sound. "I lived with an expert."

"And you still carry the scars."

"I don't carry anything," she shot back. "I was doing very well until you burst into my world. And when you go back under your rock, I'll be all right again."

He paled at her insult. For a long silent moment, he stared at her—and then let his eyes travel slowly around the room. "Is this what you call being all right?" He turned back to her, a scathing contempt twisting his mouth. "Hiding away on the top floor of a rooming house, going out with a man old enough to be your father who pats you on the hand and treats you like his daughter—and being terrified when a man comes along who might have the guts to take you to bed?"

She fought to hide the shock wave that washed over her. "I'm not—terrified. I don't—like you, that's all."

"You kissed me as if you liked me."

"I don't. You leave me cold." The lie was cool, flat.

"You little liar," he said softly. "I ought to make you eat those words."

"You couldn't."

"Are you inviting me to try?"

Her gray eyes sparkled, went luminescent with fear. "Get out of here."

"Has it occurred to you," he said, getting to his feet, towering over her, "that anyone who hates so passionately —loves just as passionately?" With the swiftness of a panther, he pulled her up out of the chair, planted his hard mouth on hers, and released her, all within the time span of an instant. She raised a hand to the mouth that tingled with the blood his kiss had brought pulsing to the surface. She said, "Was that supposed to prove something?" Each word throbbed with sarcasm.

A mocking gleam shone from his eyes. "I don't have to prove anything to you. You betray yourself every time I touch you," he said in a softly lethal tone. "Think about that. I certainly will." Before she could move or speak, he crossed the room with his long stride and let himself out the door.

She wanted to cry and scream and throw the cups at the door after him, but she didn't. Instead, she got up out of the chair, went to the door, chain-locked it, and escaped into her bedroom. Mechanically, she stepped out of her clothes and donned her nightgown, a light pink brushed cotton that she had bought for the cool nights up in the Adirondacks when she'd stayed with Dean for a month. Shaking with fear and anger and hate, she lay down on the bed. Ty Rundell was wrong about her, of course. He was a predator, a self-serving, egotistical specimen who fed on the misery of other people to make his living and, in the process, convinced himself he was some kind of grand humanist, solving the problems of the entire human race. She had seen his kind before, when she was very young, but she hadn't understood about scavengers then. She had been in awe of anyone who was creative—the writers in particular had caught her young imagination. Until she was thirteen and had stupidly confided to her mother that she thought one man in particular was "super."

The next night she had been restless, thirsty, unable to sleep, and had gotten out of bed. She had not turned on any lights, and when she reached the hall, she heard the voice of the man she had admired talking in low tones with her mother.

"Claire—my God, you're beautiful. Your breasts are ivory perfection—"

Her mother's voice had sounded cool, almost blasé. "What a way you have with words, darling. It's no wonder all the women fall for you."

"What women—" the words were half-muffled. She had crept around the corner and saw them then, her mother half lying on the cushions of the long cream sofa, her designer dress unbuttoned to the waist, her much-praised skin gleaming in the soft light of one lamp, the man Leigh had thought wonderful leaning over her, his lips pressed against an ivory breast.

The words were languidly seductive. "My understudy, for one, and my hairdresser, for another." Her mother had laughed softly. "Why, even my daughter thinks you're quite something."

"Your daughter?" He said the words as if he couldn't remember Leigh existed. Then he groaned and raised his head. "My God, you can't think I'd ever be interested in her" was the muffled answer. "She's a carbon copy, a dull child who happens to look like you. You're a beautiful, gorgeous original who has no equal."

Her mother's soft laugh had been husky, satisfied, and purring, like a cat who has captured the mouse. "I've never been with a man who could be eloquent and aroused at the same time. It's quite a novelty." The light gleamed off the golden polish of her mother's long, sleekly manicured fingernails as she threaded them through the dark strands of hair Leigh had thought so attractive. "You are—aroused, aren't you, darling?"

His groan was throaty, disturbed. "Claire. You must know what you're doing to me—"

She had crept back to her room, sickened and destroyed in a way she hardly understood. It was only years later, when her mother grew older and her fame lessened, that the obsessive need to seduce every male in sight, especially those who cast an eye over Claire's young, attractive daughter, was so evident even Leigh could see it. But that was much later. The first time, young as she was, she had understood only on a subconscious level. Careful after that night not to express admiration for any male in front of her mother, she told Claire that she, Leigh, was abnormal, that she hated men. Her mother had only laughed— but she had believed Leigh, because she wanted to. "Leigh's little hang-up" Claire labeled it, secretly delighted because it removed Leigh from the competition.

Leigh played her part well—until Dean. With him, she almost overdid it—and cheated herself out of a friend.

She and Claire had been driving through the mountains on a rare motor trip, and their car had broken down in Tupper Lake. Dean had fixed it and taken them to dinner. During the meal, Dean had to be told who Claire Foster was. That endeared him to Leigh from the first, but she told her mother she thought he was boring, and for the first time, her mother seemed to agree. But Dean's virile masculinity and his cool self-assurance had cast a potent spell over Claire. Their marriage had shocked and angered Leigh—until she discovered that Dean was as determined to accept her as the daughter he had wanted and never had as she was to push him away. For nearly a year she resisted. But in the end, her mother, bored and restless, had left—and Leigh stayed. Under a mature man's care for the first time in her life, she began to relax and enjoy the kind of loving protection that Dean's special brand of caring provided. He made it possible for her to achieve a peace within herself—and a life of her own—independent of her mother's.

Thinking about Dean, remembering the quiet times of sitting around the campfire, roasting marshmallows till they ignited, waving the fire out and pulling the sticky charred remains off the stick to eat with her fingers . . . she fell asleep.

CHAPTER THREE

It was almost one o'clock when she woke, and by the time she showered, dressed, and cleaned the apartment, it was close to three before she could sit down and relax with a cup of coffee and look over the mountain of papers she had to have ready for Monday's classes. She was halfway through the history quiz she had given on Friday when the knock sounded on her door.

She tensed, knowing Hunt would have tapped out his special little clichéd rhythm. She smoothed suddenly moist palms down the side of her denim pants, tugged her T-shirt down over her hips, and went to the door.

"Howdy." It was Deke she-couldn't-remember-his-last-name, and in his jeans and denim jacket he looked ten feet tall holding her little ice bag by its plastic neck. "Just stopped by to return this."

"Uh, thank you, Mr.—"

"Just Deke is okay." His eyes skittered past her shoulder. "Actually, I had an ulterior motive."

"Oh?" She took the ice bag from him, her face carefully expressionless.

"I was hoping I might get invited in for a cup of coffee." A grin split his wide mouth. "Figured the air might be a little better up here than it is down there." He nodded toward the stairway.

She gave him a slight smile and couldn't stop herself

from asking, "What's the matter with the air down there?"

"It's a mite blue, mostly." He shook his head, a mischievous light in his eyes. "Us gentlemanly cowboys have tender ears. We aren't used to such talk."

"I'm sure you aren't," she said dryly, knowing she was being charmed, but liking the way he was doing it. "Won't you come in—Deke?"

"Why, thank you kindly, ma'am, don't mind if I do."

She went into the kitchenette to stow away the ice bag and fill the coffee maker. "Oh, and Deke?" She turned.

He lifted an eyebrow. "Ma'am?"

"Now that you're inside, you can drop the phony cowboy act."

He grimaced. "Was it that bad?" His tone was normal, his accent middle western, she guessed.

"I've heard worse."

"How did I give myself away?"

"I heard you talk yesterday, remember?"

"God, yes." He shot her an admiring, amused smile. "That was stupid of me."

"We all make mistakes. Milk or sugar?"

"Just black."

She poured out the coffee, and he took up his cup. "Careful, it's hot," she warned him.

"Just the way I like it." He sipped it, closed his eyes appreciatively, and put the cup down.

She tasted her own and then lowered the cup to the table and said in what she hoped was a casual tone, "What seems to be the trouble—down there?"

"We both overslept—and the one mechanic in town doesn't work on Saturday afternoon. Looks like we're stuck here for the weekend."

"Looks like," she said noncommittally.

"I don't think Ty slept very well last night, either."

"Perhaps the beds weren't right for you," she said coolly.

"We've slept in worse," Deke drawled.

"I'll bet you have," she murmured.

"Hey." Deke held his hands up, palms out. "Hold your fire." His smile was rueful. "I surrender."

"Sorry. I guess I didn't sleep very well last night, either." Restlessly, she got up from the table and went to the sink to dump her coffee out. It had gotten bitter.

Deke's eyes flickered over the papers scattered at the other end of the table. "You really do—teach?"

She turned and leaned against the counter. "Well, if I'm pretending, the kids haven't noticed."

"That isn't what I meant. I—"

"Skip it. What do you do for a living, Deke? Do you work for—Mr. Rundell?"

"I suppose you could say that. Mostly I just stick around to help him keep his feet on the ground."

"Do they have—a tendency to fly off?"

Deke squinted at her, lifted a light brown eyebrow. "Yeah, once in a while he goes into orbit." He drained his coffee cup, set it back on the table. "We started out as stunt men together. He'd done some race car driving, so he did cars, and I did horses."

"Doesn't he ride? He told me he was raised on a ranch."

"He rides—but only when he has to." Deke's eyes narrowed. "When did he tell you that?"

Caught, she thought rapidly, gave up the idea of lying. "Last night. Neither one of us could sleep. We—went for a walk. More coffee?"

"I won't turn it down." He held out his cup, his brown eyes watching her. She turned her back to him to replace the coffee server, and he said carefully, "Must have been a nice night for a walk."

She faced him, leaning against the cupboard, her hands gripping the narrow edge. "It—was."

"He doesn't usually tell anybody about being raised on a ranch." Deke ducked his head, took another sip of coffee. "He make a pass at you?"

She looked at him steadily and said in a dry tone, "What do you want—a blow-by-blow—or are you watching out for Ty?"

A smile lifted his mouth, crinkled the corners of his eyes. "Ty can watch out for himself. I just wanted to know if I'm stepping on any toes, that's all. We have a rule. No poaching on the other's territory."

The thought of being just another conquest in the long line of women snared by Ty Rundell made her say icily, "I'm not—a territory."

Deke raised a lazy eyebrow. "That fellow you were with yesterday staked his claim?"

The temptation to hide behind Hunt was strong—but her innate honesty won out. "No. I don't belong to any man. I belong to myself."

"Good. Then you shouldn't have any objection if I volunteer to cook a pizza for your supper tonight."

She hadn't fallen into such a skillfully constructed trap since Paul.... "You ought to wear a sign. Posted. Dangerous."

"Now what fun would that be?" He hitched his pants up at the knee, and swung one leg over the other. "You can always refuse"—he grinned at her, a disarming, little-boy grin—"but you'll be sorry if you do. I make a mean pizza."

"There aren't any utensils in that apartment downstairs. What are you going to bake it in?"

Deke raised his eyebrows and said, "Now don't that beat all? I bought all the ingredients and forgot I didn't have anything to put them on."

His boyish air of innocence made her want to laugh. "You're a fraud, Deke."

45

His grin widened. "But you're gonna let me use your pizza pan, anyway, aren't you?"

"Tell me something."

With an extravagant wave of his hand he said, "For you, honey—anything."

"What do you do for Ty Rundell, really—besides soften up the people he's decided he needs to see?"

Deke narrowed his eyes and stared at her from under light brown lashes. "You call me dangerous? Honey, you're lethal. I never had a teacher as sharp as you."

"Probably because none of them had their early training in Hollywood," she said, her voice dry. "I used to watch a producer slap an actor on the back at a party one night and fire him the next morning."

Deke's face changed, became thoughtful. She could almost see him mulling her words over in his mind and searching for a response.

"Whatever you're going to say—make it the truth," she warned.

His face changed, seemed older, more right for him, somehow. "All right. Cards on the table." She tensed and he watched her, as if he was curious about her reaction to what he had to say. "Ty didn't order me to come up here. We don't have any grand plan. We mostly play it by ear. I know Ty wants to talk to you. He evidently didn't make much headway last night because if he had, he'd be writing this afternoon instead of swearing at everything and everybody in sight. I took it upon myself to see if I could get you to spend the evening with us."

She shook her head, and he held up his hand. "Now, wait a minute. This isn't an 'either-or' situation. I—personally—want your company this evening. Whether you want to talk to Ty or not—well, that's your business. If you don't want to talk, fine. We'll eat, instead. But don't say no to me because you aren't going to talk to Ty."

She shook her head, knowing she should say no. Instead

she said, half smiling, "You are a very persuasive and dangerous man, Deke." But he was interesting, too, and he made her realize how narrow her life had become since she'd come to Springwater. She hadn't talked with anyone like him in ages, and it was stimulating to match wits with an adept adversary. Deke reminded her of her stepfather —although she was sure Deke was far more worldly aware than Dean. Dean was intelligent and wise and thought everyone else was, too. Deke knew better. Knowledge of the world gleamed from his eyes.

She leaned back against the counter. "Pepperoni?"

Deke grinned. "You bet. Nothing else but." Pressing his advantage, he said, "Eight o'clock?"

"Come around seven thirty, and put it together here."

"You got yourself a date." Deke eased his lanky frame out of the chair.

When he was gone, she cleared the cups away from the table and ran the hot water into the sink. Was she completely insane, inviting two men into her life who could destroy the peace of mind that she had worked so hard to achieve during the last seven years? She hadn't fenced verbally with an intelligent man since the last time she was in Hollywood.

The last time. She thrust her hands into the hot water, as if to cleanse away the thoughts. They ran on inside her head, unhindered by her senses.

She was twenty when her mother called her at Dean's cabin that summer. "I've always taken such good care of myself, but—now it seems I have this tumor, darling. It's the damnedest thing." A hesitation, a slight laugh. Claire Foster, at her Academy Award best. "They say there's nothing that can be done, the fools." Another long pause while Leigh caught her breath. "I need you, darling. Will you—come?"

Reluctant, and guilty and ashamed of her reluctance, Leigh agreed. That summer, between her sophomore and junior year in college, she climbed on the plane to Los Angeles. . . . On the way she read the magazines she had brought with her, magazines about teaching and creativity and exciting new ways to present classroom material. She had a talent for working with children, she discovered, and she enjoyed her college work. She had read those instead of the glossy magazine the flight attendant handed her with a picture of her mother on the cover. That had been a mistake. For if she had read that magazine, she would have known about Paul. . . .

She sloshed the cups vigorously into the water and turned the faucet on full force to rinse them. Her legs trembled; her hands shook. She reached to set the cups out in the plastic drainer. The phone rang. She dropped the cup, watching it bounce between the rubberized prongs. The phone went again.

Like someone in a dream, she walked to the little table where the phone sat beside the sofa. "Hello?"

"Leigh? You sound strange. Is anything wrong?"

"No, nothing's wrong. How are you?" Sharp, perceptive Eve with her wasp tongue and her tall, agile body was a woman in her forties who had never found a man able—or willing—to match wits with her.

"I'm looking for company, that's how I am," she said bluntly. "These math tests are driving me bananas. I've got to get out of this house or I'll lose what little sanity I have. Are you busy tonight?"

"I—" She started to explain about Deke and the pizza—and something, some sixth sense made her stop. Suppose she tossed some of Deke's maneuvering back in his lap? She didn't want to face Ty and Deke alone, and Eve's presence would make the numbers come out right. "No, I'm not doing anything. Why don't you drop over about eight? I'm—tied up till then."

She wasn't one to tell lies or indulge in subterfuges, but

she knew if she told Eve the truth, Eve would run a mile. Eve, like Leigh, carried battle scars.

"Oh," Leigh said, "don't eat supper. We'll have something here."

"You're on," Eve answered with relish.

She felt a touch of remorse when she hung up the phone—and shrugged it away. Off guard, Eve was stunningly attractive.

Promptly at seven thirty, Deke appeared at her door. He was smiling—and he was alone.

"Ty refused to come," he told her cheerily, a big brown paper bag in his arms.

She felt a brief, unreasonable flash of irritation. For two hours she had braced herself for this encounter, and he hadn't even bothered to come. She felt as if she had been pushing against a wall that had suddenly given way. There was something else, too, the familiar feeling of being betrayed. Their walk in the darkness—and that kiss—had meant nothing to him. But even though she told herself that she was glad she wouldn't be seeing him again, she couldn't prevent herself from asking, "Where—is he?"

"Working on the car. We pushed it down to the station, and he's down there now, lying on his back, looking under the damn thing." Deke shook his head. "I told him to forget it." He smiled. "He doesn't listen to me much."

"No," she murmured, "I don't suppose he does."

She had laid everything out on the table Deke would need, a round pan, a bowl, spoons, measuring cups, a pizza cutter. He went to work at once, deftly measuring the ingredients for the crust into the bowl and dousing the flour and yeast with the warm water. He kept up a running commentary all the while, telling her about his work in the studio. He told a story well, but she listened with only half her attention, her eyes trained on the clock above the stove. Ty's absence knocked everything off center. Without him, the whole thing would look like a setup to Eve.

She would take one look—and run. Nothing Leigh might say would convince her to stay—unless she could think of something. . . .

The pizza was in the oven when the knock on her door finally came. Nervously, Leigh leaped out of the chair, aware of Deke's lazy gaze on her as she walked to the door, smoothing her hand down her denim skirt.

Eve blew in like a winter storm, breathless, in a hurry. "I didn't know what you were having to eat, so I brought some red wine. I hope that's okay—" Eve thrust the brown-wrapped bottle at her and moved to take off her khaki rain jacket—when she saw Deke. Her green eyes flew back to Leigh's, and they glistened with anger. "I thought you weren't busy," she muttered in an undertone to Leigh, fury in her tone. "I could kill you for this." Her arm went back into her jacket, and she looked over Leigh's shoulder and spoke to Deke the way she might have if he had been a stranger she had jostled in a public place. "I'm sorry. Leigh didn't tell me she had company. I'm obviously crashing the party. We'll make it some other time, Leigh," she gritted in a voice that hinted that time might never come and turned to make her escape.

Desperately, Leigh tried to think of a way to stop her—and got sudden, unexpected help. "Don't go," Deke drawled, moving away from the stove, taking a step toward them. "This isn't a private party—" he contradicted Eve persuasively, "and I did forget the wine."

"I really don't think I can stay," Eve said bluntly, protesting—but she wasn't walking out the door. Leigh watched with interest as the color climbed in her friend's cheeks.

"Don't let me chase you away. I don't bite"—his hands came out, palms up, unguarded, and the grin widened—"at least not on the first meeting."

Inwardly, Leigh groaned. That touch of sexual teasing would be just enough to send Eve flying out the door.

But Eve wasn't moving. She impaled Leigh with those green eyes and hissed at her under her breath, "You set me up for this."

Recovering, Leigh said, "I'll explain later. Please stay." She played her trump card, the one she should have played at the very beginning. "I need you."

Eve shot her a look that went straight to the jugular. Leigh fended off the sharp arrows in those flashing green eyes, shifted the bottle of wine to the crook of her arm, and stared back at her, her own gray eyes pleading. While they waged silent combat, Deke walked closer, introduced himself, and reached for Eve's coat. She handed it to him and in response to his introduction, explained she and Leigh were coworkers.

His hands rested briefly on her shoulders, ostensibly to help her with her jacket. Eve's cheeks brightened more than ever. Her movements were always quick, graceful, but she was even quicker getting out of her jacket. She shrugged it off in two seconds flat.

Deke hung Eve's jacket in the closet near the door. Leigh turned away, opened the wine, went to the cabinet, and got out the wineglasses, leaving Eve and Deke to stand on the other side of the room gazing at each other, Deke with interest, Eve with barely contained anger. Leigh poured out the dark, glossy liquid and crossed the room to hand a glass to Eve. "Sit down," she said, indicating the sofa. Eve went to one corner and sank down into the cushions nervously, like a cat on the defensive.

"Deke was a stunt man in Hollywood."

Eve tried not to be impressed. "Sounds dangerous." She sipped her wine carefully.

Deke lowered himself into the sofa on the opposite end, a comfortable distance away from Eve. Leigh sank into a chair across from him, congratulating herself. Eve wasn't happy—but she was here.

He said, "It's probably not any more dangerous than what you do—facing an unruly mob of kids."

Eve's eyes flickered under black lashes. "There are some days when I'd agree with that a hundred percent. What kind of stunts do you do, Mr. Slayton?"

"Deke, ma'am," he corrected her gently. "I'm out of the business now, but when I was in it, I did the horse stunts mostly. I grew up on the rodeo circuit. My father and brothers were all performers."

"Are they in Hollywood, too?"

Deke sipped his wine, closed his eyes in appreciation for the taste. Then he looked at Eve. "No. They all had more sense. I ended up in glittertown because of my wife."

Eve stiffened, then relaxed. "You're married."

"Was," Deke said softly. "She was killed three years ago in an accident on the freeway." He looked down, studying his wine, his face dark. "She always worried about me getting it at work." He raised his head, looked at Eve. "Funny how things turn out sometimes."

"Yes, it is," Eve agreed, her voice soft. "I'm sorry."

"Yeah. So am I. I've never stopped being sorry." Deke lifted his wineglass to his lips.

There was a little silence, and then Leigh, too, lifted her glass, sipped. Only someone with the hide of an elephant would have been unaffected by the bitter regret in Deke's voice, and Eve did not have the hide of an elephant. Leigh saw her mouth soften, her eyes lose their angry, defensive look.

The pizza was warm and rich with tomato sauce, cheese, and pepperoni, and after they had eaten, Eve leaned back in her chair and looked almost normal. The meal had been punctuated by congenial conversation and occasional bursts of laughter, and her face was flushed from the wine, her eyes sparkling.

She plied Deke with questions about the movies and doing stunts, and he answered each one thoughtfully.

"A stunt man has to know a lot more about filming than just being able to jump through a window. He has to know about camera shots and lenses and the way a set is built, or he might end up doing his stunt 'off camera' and have to do it again because he missed the big eye. Though he isn't considered an actor and doesn't use an agent, he is a double, and he still has to know how to act. He has to take that fall or handle that horse in a way that convinces the viewer he is the actor he's doubling for."

"You said your specialty was horses," Leigh said, relaxing back against the sofa cushion.

"Most stunt men don't like working with horses. They'd rather ride a car into a wall. Not me. I'll take a horse any day. Trouble with a horse is—most of them are too smart to ride into trouble. They can see it coming, and they back off. You gotta know that about horses or you can't work with them. Ty hated the horses. He did cars—and stunts that involved fire."

The lovely euphoria that had surrounded Leigh fell away. "Fire—"

"Yeah, sure. Chances are if you saw a man on fire from his head to his heels in a film, it was Ty."

She felt a sharp stab of anxiety. "He doesn't—do that anymore, does he?"

"No," Deke drawled, "he doesn't do that anymore." A tiny gleam lit his eyes.

"Why did you do it?" Eve asked, watching him.

Deke shrugged. "With me, I just kind of fell into it." He grinned. "No pun intended. I suppose I did it for the same reason anybody risks life and limb unnecessarily—just to see if you can flirt with death and win. Somehow—you always feel more alive afterwards—as if you were clean inside. It's the adrenaline, they say."

Eve shuddered. "I'll certainly pay more attention to those people I see in the movies hanging around on the side of a mountain after this."

"Ah," Deke said softly, "but if you notice us, it means we aren't doing the job correctly."

"It's just plain stupid for a man to risk his life like that," Leigh burst out.

Deke looked at her, his eyes narrowing. "There are stunt women, too, plenty of them. There's a whole organization."

"I'm glad," Leigh said coolly. "More coffee?"

Deke frowned, slid back the cuff of his blue plaid shirt, looked at his watch. "Guess I'll go on back and see what Ty's up to. Thank you for the company."

"Thank you for the pizza," Leigh said hastily, getting to her feet.

"My pleasure." With the agile grace of an athlete, Deke got to his feet. At the door, he turned and looked at Eve. "Since it looks like we'll be stranded here for a couple of days, I may see you again."

"I suppose that's—possible," Eve said lightly, gazing up at him.

"Well—good-night," Deke said, dipping his head.

When he had closed the door and Eve heard the second riser creak, she said dryly, "Thanks a lot—friend."

Leigh got to her feet and began to pick up the wineglasses and coffee cups. "You're welcome."

"Well, don't just scurry around here like Mrs. Goodhousekeeper. Give. Tell."

"What's to tell?"

"You might start with where you met him and end with why you dragged me into this."

"You heard about the car that lost its brakes yesterday —it was driven by his friend. They'll have to wait till Monday to get their car fixed, and they've rented the apartment below. That's all there is to it."

"What are Hollywood stunt men doing in Springwater?"

"Looking for material for a book, so they say."

"In Springwater? That doesn't make any sense."

It did, of course, but Leigh couldn't explain. She had told no one in Springwater of her background, not even Eve. She made her shrug casual. "People from the entertainment world don't have to make sense, do they?"

"Hey, don't kid yourself. They're out to make a buck just like all the rest of us. And I don't think there are many bucks to be made in Springwater."

Eve's words stung, but Leigh went on tidying up the apartment, trying to hide her distress under a calm, smooth face. Eve was only saying what she knew to be true, but somehow it hurt more to hear it from her best friend. When she picked up the ashtray that Deke had used, she saw that he had left his packet of tobacco lying beside it. "Perhaps when you see Deke again, you can ask him about it."

"I won't be seeing him again, and you know it. Men like that aren't interested in single, independent schoolteachers."

"You forgot the glasses bit."

"With glasses," Eve added caustically. She put her hands on the sofa cushions and pushed herself to her feet. "Well, thank you for a most instructive evening, Miss Carlow. I learned more about movie stunts than I ever wanted to know."

Leigh turned, frowned. "That's not fair and you know it. You enjoyed listening to him."

Eve bent over to pick up her purse and with the easy familiarity of many visits, went to the closet to get her coat. "Too much," she said huskily. "I'd stay and help you with the dishes—but you deserve some kind of penitence."

"Eve—"

"Don't say it," she warned. "I'm too old and too smart to believe a lie. See you Monday morning."

She went out the door, leaving Leigh standing there

looking after her, wondering if she, too, was too old and too smart to believe a lie.

"Have a good time?" Ty heard the ill humor in his voice, saw that Deke heard it too, and cursed himself for a fool. Deke stepped into the apartment, closed the door behind him, dropped his denim jacket on the back of a chair, and carefully avoided looking at Ty, who was sprawled out on the dark green lounging chair, his feet lifted off the floor, papers spread over his lean legs, a pen in his hand, his dark hair tousled as if he had run his fingers through it frequently.

Deke calculated the odds, decided to live dangerously. "As a matter of fact I did," he drawled. "Best evening I've had in a long time." He took off his boots, flopped down on one of the double beds, stretched out with his head on the pillow, his hands folded under his neck—and waited.

Ty looked down at his papers and scowled. "Save me anything to eat?"

"Nope." Deke was complacent. "We ate it all, every last crumb."

"Took you all this time to eat one pizza?"

"No—" Deke let the word linger. "We—got acquainted"—knowing full well he was being dishonest by omitting mention of Eve's presence. But he was curious. Leigh's reaction to the news that Ty had done dangerous stunts with fire had been interesting. He'd do a little more probing.

There was a long, drawn-out silence. "Make any headway with her?" Ty's voice had a muffled, almost strangled sound.

"Kinda hard to tell at this point, wouldn't you say?" He purposely walked closer to disaster. "What did you find out about the car?"

"Brake line is rusted through. Must have been that water I had sloshing around inside the back footwell when

I was in New York last March and didn't discover till I started back to California."

"How long will it take to get it fixed?"

"God knows. Why?" The word was a short, pointed dagger.

Deke went over the precipice. "Just wondered how much time I had to—?"

The bottom part of the lounge chair snapped down. Ty twisted his head and glared at Deke. "Dammit, leave her alone."

"Hey." Deke held up his hands in mock surprise. "You gave me the impression you weren't interested."

"I—wasn't." The words were ground out.

"Sounds like you've changed your mind."

"Maybe I have. Just stay away from her while I'm deciding, okay?"

"She's not your usual—style"—Deke stifled a grin—"especially with those health shoes and that hair tied back in a bun." Deke closed his eyes to shut out the look of fury that was darkening Ty's face. "You should have seen it tonight. That hair glows from the inside, like honey held up to the sun. I wonder what it feels like to run it through your fingers. . . ."

Ty shot to his feet, the papers on his lap scattering around him like leaves. They fluttered to the floor, white scraps of refuse that Ty stepped over as he went to the closet.

"Going somewhere?" Deke asked silkily, turning his head, watching Ty thrust his arms into his jacket.

"Yeah," Ty growled. "Out to look for some peace and quiet."

Deke closed his eyes and laid his head back down on the pillow. "Don't slam the door when you go, will you?"

Ty's answer was to close the door with a violent silence that told Deke he had stretched friendship to its far limits.

CHAPTER FOUR

Ty wasn't sure at first what had dragged him up out of sleep. He came to consciousness reluctantly. Then he heard them, the clear chiming of church bells. He had never before heard a bell ring with such vigor. He could almost see the small boy who must be pulling on the rope to make the sound echo against the hills with such repeated joyousness. He lay still, listening, feeling the disconsonant, yet melodious clang resound to the core of his being.

Those church bells were a part of Leigh Carlow's life. She had heard them every Sunday since when? Five years ago? Yes, that was what Dean had said. She's been in Springwater five years. And during that time she had not become engaged or married.

God, he had to stop thinking about her. But he couldn't. He'd prowled restlessly through Springwater last night, walking for hours until he was exhausted, in an attempt to put her out of his mind. It hadn't worked. He seemed to be obsessed with her, had been from the moment he looked at those pictures of her with her mother. Those pictures had goaded him into driving miles into the Adirondacks to ask Dean endless questions—including the one about men. "Haven't there been any men in her life, any love affairs?"

Dean had given him a straight look. "She'll have to answer that question for you. I can't."

Ty had felt a rough impatience at the man's protectiveness, but now, seeing Leigh, he understood it. Outwardly, she was cool, self-contained. But there was a vulnerability about her that made him ache to know her, get inside her head. *Anything else?* his mocking mind muttered. No, dammit, no. That "anything else" was out of the question. He'd kissed her, sure. But he couldn't get involved with her. She was out of his reach—a million miles out of his world. They had nothing in common. She hated the entertainment world; he made his living in it. She seemed happy to live her life in this rural bliss; he would go crazy here in a matter of days.

A matter of days. By Monday, possibly Tuesday at the latest, he would be out of here. All he had to do was retain his hold on reality till then. Once he went back to California and started research on another celebrity's child, he would forget her.

He listened to Deke's heavy, even breathing. He'd been a fool to let Deke get under his skin last night. He just hadn't wanted to see Deke get involved, that was all. At least he, Ty, had showed some sense. He'd stayed away. That was the only thing to do, stay away. He'd tell her he was no longer interested in interviewing her and he'd get the car fixed and he'd get the hell out. He was a sensible, logical man, and he'd never yet lost his head over a woman. He wasn't about to start now.

If only those bells would stop ringing, maybe he could quit thinking about her—about how he wanted her like hell, more every time he saw her, how he wanted to possess that cool mouth again and make it pulse with warmth, how he wanted to run his hands over her slim body and discover its secret, sensitive places, and make love to her again and again. . . . He threw back the covers, glancing over at the still-sleeping Deke. He had to do something to divert his mind: write, work. Then later—he'd go see her, tell her he was no longer interested in interviewing her. She would no doubt be relieved, and he would be, too.

Then why wasn't he? Why did he feel irritated and restless? It must be because he was anxious to get out of Springwater. . . .

When Leigh Carlow stepped out of the church door, the breeze caught at her yellow hat. She reached up and clutched at the brim, holding it with slender fingers as she walked down the sidewalk, her high-heeled pumps making her body sway with a willowy grace in the yellow linen suit she wore. The sun had risen bright and warm, and she wore no coat.

"Leigh, darling."

She turned. From the group of people who were clustered in the autumn sunshine there in the front of the church, Hunt, looking much slimmer in his dark navy suit than he had in his costume Friday night, stepped out and grasped her elbow. "How are you?"

"Fine. I didn't see you in church," she said, more for something to say than anything else.

He seemed taken aback. "I sat where I always do. Strange you didn't see me." He frowned for a moment, and then his face cleared. "All right if I stop by this afternoon and pick up your costume?"

"Yes, of course."

"Good. See you later, darling. Got to run." He leaned forward to kiss her cheek, and she caught the scent of his cologne, a cloying, spicy scent. He wore a different scent to school during the week. He walked away and left her standing there, making her realize how overpowering his cologne was. The scent of another man drifted through her mind, a clean, masculine smell mingled with the smoky aroma of a fall night crisp with stars. . . .

"Going out with Hunt tonight?" Eve stood beside her, tall and slender in a silky green dress, her short black hair blowing around her head.

"No. Were you coming over?"

"No," Eve echoed, her face wry. "I'm not coming over."

"You sound positively unfriendly this morning," Leigh murmured.

"You're lucky I'm speaking to you." There was a feverish brightness around Eve's eyes, as if she had hardly slept last night.

"I needed moral support," Leigh said blandly.

"Well, get your morals supported somewhere else after this, okay? Good old reliable Eve is no longer available as a port in a storm."

The waspishness in her words rolled harmlessly off Leigh. She had known Eve too long and they had shared too much for her to be offended. She knew that Eve was running scared.

"Remember what I said," Eve cautioned, patting her arm, her gesture at complete variance with her words. "A friend indeed is a friend who leaves a friend alone."

Leigh kept her face expressionless. "I can take a hint."

"Just until Buck Rogers leaves town, okay?"

Leigh laughed and tilted her head up under her hat, still holding the brim. "Roy Rogers was the cowboy. Buck Rogers was a space hero."

"Ranch, galaxy, who cares where he came from? Just so he goes away. And soon. Until then, you don't know me."

A smile lingered on Leigh's mouth. "What a fair-weather friend you turned out to be."

"You guessed it. Thank goodness you're smart as well as beautiful. See you in school."

Eve turned and left, the green silk fluttering around her legs. Leigh watched her go, her mouth lifted in a wry smile. Eve was her own woman, and you had to take her or leave her as she was.

After saying "good morning" to several of the parents and a few of her students, Leigh turned for home. She hadn't bothered to drive; she had walked to church, and now she set off, her heels clipping rhythmically on the sidewalk. The breeze died down, and she took off her hat and lengthened her stride, enjoying the feeling of walking in the warm sunshine. The blue sky and the hills mottled with splotches of red-orange maples and dark green pines gave her a feeling of well-being. She strode along purposefully, and it was almost with a sense of regret that she reached the house and climbed the four steps to Viola's porch.

She saw him through the inside door. The old-fashioned oval glass flashed a close-up view of Ty Rundell's face turned in profile, his dark head of hair full and vibrant, his arm clad in the oxblood leather jacket extended toward the door latch. Then he turned his head—and saw her.

The sight of her punched the breath from his lungs. She was a vision of grace and movement, clad in yellow, her honey hair flying free around her face and shoulders. There was a freshness about her, an unstudied grace in the way she walked up the stairs that was utterly feminine—utterly destroying. The sensible thoughts, the cool decision to put her out of his mind and leave . . . fled. All that remained was a driving compulsion to talk to her, to be with her—and to possess her.

Stunned, Leigh stood and stared at their merging reflections. Her hair disheveled by the breeze, her cheeks flushed from the fresh air, the yellow suit she wore made a ghost image that played over the glass-distorted view of his. It was as if their two separate bodies, male and female, were merging on another plane. . . . Her skin prickled with a fey sense of alarm.

That tingle of awareness crawled down her spine and sensitized her to everything about him. His pupils changed, flared darkly with an emotion she couldn't identify. Framed in the oval of wood, the dark, cynical face and well-cut controlled mouth hardened, and the black silky lashes dropped down. Whatever it was he was feeling, he didn't want her to see it. What was it? Contempt—or merely disappointment that she hadn't succumbed to his charm?

Bitterly aware of an inner struggle of her own, she stiffened and took an instinctive step backwards, away from him. He pushed the door open and stepped out onto the porch. Deke followed, looking sleepy but familiar in his blue denim jacket, jeans, and leather boots.

Ty said, "Good morning."

His voice was low, the timbre disturbingly sensual, too much a reminder of the words he had muttered in her ear and the kiss they had shared in the dark before the dawn. . . . "Hello." The word seemed to stick in her throat.

"Morning, Leigh. Beautiful morning, isn't it?" Deke's voice had a cheerful, nonthreatening sound about it. She relaxed slightly and smiled at him. "Yes, it is." The breeze freshened, and she reached up and brushed back a strand of hair that floated across her cheek.

Ty took a step away from her and thrust his hand into one of his pants pockets, as if he were anxious to go. Deke shot him a sidelong glance and then turned to Leigh. "I left my tobacco pouch in your apartment last night. We were going out to buy another, but if you're going right up—"

"Yes, yes, I am. I—did find it, and I came down with it before I went to church, but your apartment was—quiet. I didn't want to disturb you."

"We slept late this morning—at least, I did." To Ty, he said, "You were up working though when I got up."

Ty said coolly, "I had some ideas I wanted to get down on paper."

There was an odd silence. Self-consciously, Leigh pushed another errant strand of hair away from her face. Ty made a restless movement, and Leigh felt her temper flare. He couldn't wait to be on his way. That stung. She clamped down on her irritation and said crisply to Deke, "I'll go up and get your pouch."

"I'll come with you," Deke said quickly. "You coming, Ty?"

"No. I'm going to go take another look at the car. You can catch up with me later."

She climbed the stairs ahead of Deke, fighting to control her annoyance. It had been on the tip of her tongue to invite them both in for coffee and a sweet roll, but now she was glad she hadn't given in to the impulse. Ty Rundell was an arrogant man who didn't even have the decency to be civil now that he had no further use for her.

She unlocked the door and crossed to the table where she had left Deke's pouch, picked it up, and handed it to him.

"Thank you," he said. "I'm not usually so careless."

"Maybe you had other things on your mind last night."

"Maybe I did." He stood for a moment, just holding the tobacco pouch, staring down at it. "Ty will probably be working all afternoon. Think Eve would throw me out if I went around to see her?"

"Chances are she will," Leigh said steadily. She studied his face, then smiled. "But an old stunt man like you should be able to take a fall or two and bounce right back, shouldn't you?"

Deke grinned back at her. "You think so? I don't know. My timing might be off."

"She lives at the end of this cross street on the edge of the creek in a small white house. You can't miss it."

Deke's smile widened. "Thanks." Again there was a silence. Then he said easily, "Ty's not usually so brusque."

"Isn't he?" She laid her hat on the table and turned. "You don't have to apologize for him. He's a grown man. He's responsible for himself."

Deke's shoulders moved under the faded denim. "Maybe, maybe not." He studied her for a long moment, until Leigh wished heartily that he would take his pouch and go. He was far too perceptive. "We're all responsible for each other in one way or another."

"Are we?" she shot back without thinking.

Their eyes locked for a long moment before Deke's flickered away. "Yeah, I think so." Then he said in a light tone, "Good-bye, Leigh." He lifted the little pouch. "Thanks for not smoking my tobacco." His grin was irrepressible.

She smiled back at him. "No problem; anytime. Goodbye, Deke."

He pivoted and left, his closing of her door creating a poignant silence in the apartment.

For a long moment she stood staring after him. No, it couldn't be. Whatever Deke had meant about shared responsibility, he couldn't have been directing it at her. Determined to shake off her edginess, she went into her bedroom to change into jeans and a cotton blouse. She went back out to the kitchenette and ate a light lunch while correcting papers, but her gaze kept drifting away to the sunshiny view outside her skylight windows. When she found the fifth wrong answer to the same question, she knew it was because she had worded the question poorly, and she threw down her red pen in disgust, her restless mood returning with a vengeance.

She got up from her chair and paced around the room. The long, slanted windows offered a full view of the drooping willow tree, and her thoughts churned on, serving up the feel of Ty Rundell's arms around her body, his lips on hers. He had made her feel emotions she vowed she would never feel again.... She whirled around and went into her bedroom to snatch up a navy sweater. Tossing it over her shoulder with hasty grace, she went to her door and escaped through it, closing the self-locking latch behind her. She ran down the top flight of stairs, turned the corner of the landing—and nearly knocked him down.

The brush of that hard lean body against her own was bad enough. The scent of good leather and sun-tossed hair and clean man nearly unhinged her. She thrust herself backwards, her palms missing the edges of his open jacket to come in direct contact with T-shirt-covered hard, male flesh. "I'm sorry," she said instantly, dropping her hands. She took another step back and watched him, her eyes wary as a cat's.

The five-foot-square space of the landing shrunk. The wind had plucked at his dark, full head of hair, rearranging it in a style that framed his head. The crystal-clear blue eyes were more vividly blue in the tanned face, the mobile mouth lifted slightly in a faint smile. Why was he here? He was supposed to be fixing his car.

He said, "Where are you going in such a hurry?"

"I . . . Out in the country."

He stretched out a hand and leaned against the opposite wall, trapping her on the landing. She fought the rise of awareness of him, the lean line of his throat, the way his belt circled a narrow waist, the taut muscles of thigh and leg covered by faded denim.

He studied her as if he were assessing her reaction to him. She fought to keep her face cool and force her breathing to a more normal rate, but her attempt to disguise her disturbed state must have been patently obvious to him. A lazy, self-assured smile tugged at his mouth. He asked, "Are you going by yourself?"

She bit her lower lip. She didn't owe him any explanation. She found herself giving it anyway. Anything to get him to move. "Yes. I'm going to collect a corn shock and some pumpkins to decorate my room at school."

The smile drifted upward a fraction of an inch. "Is that what everybody does in Springwater on a Sunday afternoon?"

"No, mostly they set up their antique shops and"—her eyes flashed a warning—"hope some city person comes along who will buy a horse hame or a spinning wheel or an old book."

Ty lifted an eyebrow. "Rampant tourism," he said dryly.

The thought of Springwater being a tourist center made her mouth relax into a slight smile. "That's stretching it a little."

"Where are you going to get these—decorative items?"

"Out to the farm where one of my students lives."

"Won't you need some help?"

The slight softening in her manner vanished. "No. I can handle it."

The arm didn't move. "So you're going to send me up to my room to spend this beautiful day in solitary confinement."

Pushed, her gray eyes gleamed with antagonism. "You had things to do this morning," she said coolly. "I'm sure you'll find something to keep you occupied this afternoon."

He stared at her, his eyes speculative. Then he smiled, a warm, teasing smile. For some reason, her cool words had pleased him. "This morning I had other things on my mind."

The words were low, lazy, and they goaded her into action. She moved forward, thinking he would step aside to let her pass. He didn't. His body tensed and his arm tightened. She had only succeeded in putting herself right under his nose. Hastily, she stepped backward.

His eyes narrowed and a frown brought his brows together, but he didn't say anything.

In a frosty tone, she said, "Would you let me by, please?"

He settled one shoulder against the wall and flattened his palm out on the other one as if he were a permanent wedge. "Why don't I go along and give you a hand at 'bringing in the sheaves'?"

67

She met his eyes with a cool, steady look. "I'm not going to grant you an interview, Mr. Rundell."

If he felt a reaction, he hid it. He gave a careless shrug with the shoulder of the arm that was free. "That's your privilege."

"You—don't—care?"

"I decided this morning I was no longer interested in using you."

His quiet words shook her. She had not expected him to give up so easily. It was totally out of character. An unpleasant feeling made her stomach churn, a feeling she couldn't identify. It must be shock. He had surprised her, thrown her off guard. It was like lunging at a door and having it give way in front of her, leaving her stumbling, trying to regain her balance. She let her eyes flicker over his face, wondering if he really meant it. If he did, she should have been relieved. Then why was she feeling this vague sense of dissatisfaction? "Then there really isn't any point in our spending time together, is there?" She moved as if to walk past him.

He stood rock hard, unyielding. "Oh, there's a point," he drawled. "The other night proved that."

"You flatter yourself," she said bluntly.

He jerked his arm away from the wall and clasped her upper arms, his tan cheeks darkening with angry color. "Stop pretending with me, Leigh. You're as attracted to me as I am to you—"

She glared up at him. The contact of those lean fingers through the thin cotton of her blouse made her nerves sing with excitement. "Take your hands off of me."

"Dammit, woman, listen to me. There isn't much time—"

"There isn't any time—now—or ever." Her cold tone made him stare blackly at her, the small muscle on the side of his cheek working as if he were gritting his teeth. The silence teemed with unspoken, angry words. His face hardened, his mouth tightened, and the square jaw jutted out at a stubborn angle. His fingers gripped her arms, and she could almost see the internal struggle going on. What did he think he could do to her? She lifted her chin and met his gaze defiantly, fighting off the awareness that told her of a ruthless determination, a drive that had sent him to the top of his profession by his mid-thirties, a vital, relentless energy that was a force to be reckoned with.

Another long, tense moment rang in her ears. When she thought she could bear it no longer, a cool blank look shuttered his face, and he let his hands fall away. With a sardonic lift of his brow, he stepped aside.

She stood for a moment, shocked by his retreat. She had braced herself for—what? She didn't dare to think. She gathered herself and slipped past him to fly down the stairs, her heart thumping. It was only after she got into the car and drove up the steep hill out of Springwater that her breathing slowed and her heart resumed its normal pace.

Ten minutes later she pulled off the road and into the gravel driveway that curved in front of a low, white farmhouse. A maple tree in the yard had turned cherry red, its umbrella of leaves shimmering like a blaze of fire. Saucers of white Queen Anne's lace dotted the yard between the house and the barn, and when she got out of the car, she could hear the hum of bees as they gathered the last of summer's nectar.

Stan Fielding, his rounded figure clad in overalls, sauntered toward her from the back door of the house. "Finally come to collect those stalks of corn, did you?"

She nodded and got out of the car, feeling a sense of relief at being here in this sun-splashed hill country. Stan, like her stepfather, Dean, clung to the land. He drove forty miles to work every day in the city in order to live on this eighty-acre farm tucked against the hills. He kept a small herd of milking cows, black-and-white Holsteins, and a few feeder cattle, red Herefords. She could see them grazing in the hilly pasture above her.

"I didn't cut it 'cause I wasn't sure when you'd be out to get it." He cast a look back at the house, and she knew she had interrupted his late Sunday dinner.

"If you give me the corn knife, I can do it."

Stan gazed off at a distant hill, squinting. "I just sharpened it. Sure you won't cut your leg off?"

Leigh's mouth quirked. "I'm sure."

Stan thought it over for another minute, his lips pursed, his hand rubbing his cheek.

"I caught you in the middle of Sunday dinner, didn't I?" she prodded softly.

He nodded. "Will you come in and have some pumpkin pie?"

She smiled. "No, thanks. You'd better go on back and have your share before that teenage boy of yours eats it all. I can manage."

He squinted, thought, tugged at an earlobe. She had seen Tom Fielding, his son, do the same thing when he was trying to puzzle out an answer in her class.

"Okay. Just be careful, you hear?"

She stifled a smile. "I hear."

He walked away in the direction of the barn and returned in a few minutes carrying the long-handled knife. The blade itself was dark with use, but the cutting edge shone with a bright, lethally sharp glitter.

"See that edge?" He tilted his head, looking at her. "Now mind what I said, Miss Carlow."

"I understand. I'll be careful. Thanks." She started to go, then turned back. "Stan, I'll probably need twenty stalks."

"Take as much as you want," he said, favoring her with a slow smile. "Cows won't miss the little bit you need. At least you asked. Some folks don't." He gave her directions to the stand of corn he wanted her to use and handed her

70

the knife. She took it from him, trying to disguise the shock she felt as its heavy weight dragged her arm down. She clamped a firmer grip around the black tape-wrapped handle, thanked him, and turned back to her car.

At the end of the driveway she waited for a car to pass and then pulled out on the road.

Five minutes later she pulled over onto the grassy shoulder, got out, walked to the wire fence, and swung her leg over. Her graceful stride took her across the stubble, the brittle stocks making crackling sounds under her sneakers.

She reached the standing corn. Long fan leaves rattled together in dry protest. No longer green, the stalks were shades of beige and brown, streaked like wood and ringed like jungle vines. The tassels whispered in the breeze.

Might as well start bringing in the sheaves.

The low husky words shivered through her mind. She had remembered what he had said, and her mind had served it up to her in an unguarded moment. She cursed under her breath. He had no place in her life. What he said or thought made no difference to her. The soft rustle of the corn leaves turned faintly mocking.

Goaded by the need to forget Ty Rundell's voice, she tramped into the corn and seized the nearest stalk just below the tassel, showering seeds over her hand and down her arm. She ignored their tickling brush and swung at the bottom of the stalk. With one quick slice, she separated stalk from root with speedy efficiency and tossed it to the ground.

"Remind me never to accost you in a dark alley."

The voice that had been in her head was in her ears. She started in surprise and whirled around. Ty stood a foot away, his black hair catching the gleam of the sun. He had shed his jacket and changed clothes. He wore jeans that would have rivaled Deke's for longevity and a white shirt open at the throat with the cuffs rolled back, and he looked amused, relaxed, and far from the furious man she had left on the landing only moments ago. Why hadn't she heard his approach? And how had he known exactly where to find her?

Her eyes flickered past him to the sporty white Trans Am parked just behind her car. It was Eve's. Her friend had not only loaned Ty her car, she had directed him straight to Stan Fielding, no doubt.

"She said she owed you one. She said you'd know what she meant. I have a hunch you do." He gave her a lazy, considering glance that flickered down the length of the corn knife. "Are you going to use that on me?" He took a step forward.

The feeling of unreality vanished. "Don't be ridiculous."

"Would it offend your feminist sensibilities if I offered to help?" He nodded at the corn.

She hesitated, vacillating. Common sense told her he wasn't going to go away, and she'd be much more comfortable if he was cutting the corn rather than watching her do it. "As long as you're here, you may as well make yourself useful."

He seemed mildly surprised, the amused smile still curving his lips as he stepped forward. She let the knife dangle down and offered it to him handle up.

His fingers closed over hers momentarily before he lifted the knife away, reminding her that those same warm male fingers had clasped her in the cool early morning and pulled her close. . . .

If he noticed her slight stiffening, he made no sign. A lithe movement turned him toward the corn, and with a supple grace, he bent and slashed the stalk, catching it as it fell. He cut down another and another, the slight whistle of air against blade followed by the crack of steel against stalk. The play of his muscles under the white shirt was disturbing, but not any more so than the stance of his legs, slightly spread to give him balance as he swung, or the press of his firm, rounded buttocks against the well-worn denim as he leaned over to pick up each stalk and toss it on the growing pile.

When he had done several, he turned to her. "Were you planning to have me fell the rest of the field?"

She dropped her gaze to the heaped pile, her cheeks flushed. She'd forgotten to count. "No, that should be enough."

In one smooth motion, he handed her the knife, scooped up the mound of stalks, and began to walk in front of her toward the fence line, his hips moving easily, a muscular grace and strength obvious in every step he took. She hesitated for a moment and then fell in behind him, trying desperately to look away from that lithe male figure.

At the fence line he stopped and waited. She understood his unspoken request and walked around him to press the fence down with her foot. Even with his burden of corn, he swung over the low barrier easily. At the car he said, "Where do you want these?"

"In the trunk. Just a minute, I have to unlock it." She dug in the pocket of her jeans and found the key, conscious that her action had tautened the denim across her hips and that he watched with evident male enjoyment as she took the key out and bent to unlock the car.

The corn did not fit into the trunk, of course, but Ty bent his dark head and ducked under the lid to readjust the mound so that just the tassels protruded. He straightened. Tiny flecks of corn tassel and dried leaves clung to his white shirt. She had the insane urge to reach out and brush them off. "Where are you going now?"

"To the schoolhouse." Her voice was cool, cooler than she had ever believed it could be. His physical presence had intensified the heat of the sun, and perspiration trickled down her back.

"I'll come and help you."

She brushed a strand of honey-colored hair away from her cheek and faced him, her head high. "I don't need help."

He stretched out an arm and leaned on the roof of her car, the gesture vaguely reminiscent of the way he had trapped her on the stairwell, and he smiled at her with the lazy smile of a large cat after a full meal. "What do I have to do to convince you that I'm not going to pry into your private life and make it public?"

She couldn't listen to those seductive words. She might begin to believe them. "Nothing. You're wasting your time trying."

He shrugged. "I seem to have plenty to spare right now."

The movement of his shoulder sent a brown tassel seed tumbling down the front of his shirt. Her throat tightened. She forced herself to say crisply, "Well, I don't. Now, if you don't mind, I'd like to go."

He didn't move. "I don't even get a word of thanks?"

She opened the door and faced him across the top of the car, her golden lashes dropping down to block out the potent attraction of that lean face with its well-shaped mouth. "Thank you."

A faintly sardonic smile and a mocking lift of a dark brow was his answer. The piercing gaze of those keen blue eyes made her duck her head and get inside her car. Breath held, not knowing what to expect, she started the engine. To her surprise, he stepped away. She drove up to another farm driveway, made a U-turn, and accelerated past him. He wasn't looking at her. He was getting into Eve's car. He had, at last, given up on her. She relaxed until she saw the white car turn and follow her. Her heart thumped wildly.

She told herself she was being foolish. After all, they were both going to the same place. But when she drove through Springwater and climbed the hill to her destination, he was still following her.

She pulled up in front of the schoolhouse. The two-story red brick building was shaded by four tall maples clustered on the west side, but on the east a low, modern elementary wing had been attached.

She parked the car and took the keys from the ignition, only too aware that Ty Rundell had pulled up behind her. She would ignore him, go and unlock both of the double doors, then come back and get the corn and drag it up the two flights of stairs to her room. After all, what could he do to stop her?

She had underestimated him. When she returned and unlocked the trunk, he walked up and scooped the bundle into his arms from under her nose.

"Lead the way," he said, and when she frowned and shook her head, he muttered, "There's no use in both of us getting covered with corn leaves." He held the awkward bundle and gazed at her coolly, his determination apparent. There was nothing to do but obey.

"My God," he muttered when she unlocked the door and they entered the building. "I remember that smell. Chalk dust and pencils and industrial cleaner, and old sneakers moldering away in a locker somewhere."

A smile tugged at her lips. She began to climb the stairs, and Ty followed, his feet making solid sounds on the steps, the rustle of the corn leaves reminding her how close he was behind and making her smile fade.

She unlocked her door. The sun-warmed room was close, stifling, the smell of chalk dust even more pronounced. She gestured toward the far corner of the window wall behind the rows of desks. "You can put them there."

She went to open a window, and Ty knelt and laid his burden on the floor with as little jarring as possible. When she turned, he had straightened and was brushing the clinging bits from his arms. "What are you going to do with those?" His tone was mildly curious.

"Make a corn shock," she told him crisply.

"Need some help?" His head was bent, his eyes searching out more unwanted seeds and leaves. The sunlight from the windows gleamed on his black hair and highlighted its sheen. A dried leaf, its edges jagged, lay just at the top of his crown. Her hand made a small betraying movement. She remembered touching those black vibrant strands, remembered how her fingers had tingled with sensual pleasure. . . .

Her arm rigid with control, she jammed her hand in her pocket. "I can manage," she said in a tight voice.

Luckily, he wasn't looking at her. The dark head lifted, turned, his eyes sweeping the room. They lingered briefly on the elaborate bulletin board display, swept over the washed, green chalk board, and swung to the table where the things she had bought Friday lay, the coiled hemp rope to tie the shock, the paper cutouts of zany Halloween creatures to decorate it.

He nodded toward the rope. "Looks like you're all ready. Might as well get this started." He nodded at the pile. "I'll hold, you stack."

He leaned over the stalks and picked them up one by one, holding them upright until he was almost hidden and the bundle in his arms was so big that he couldn't bend over it. "Hand me some more, will you?"

She hung on the edge of a decision. She didn't want him here, didn't want his help. But standing behind that bundle of dried corn, he looked very human. She felt her mouth curving at the sight of the glossy hair being showered once more by dry leaves. His utterly unselfconscious attitude about his appearance disarmed her. It didn't matter to him that he looked more like a farmer every minute. The sophisticated Hollywood producer had vanished. She had a feeling she was glimpsing a warm, deeply intelligent personality, a man who had not lost his perspective. He was completely lacking in a sense of self-importance.

He flicked an impatient, bright-eyed look at her. "Well, come on, lady, lend a hand. I'm not your private scarecrow."

She laughed, the wry words increasing her liking for him. "I'm sure every girl in junior high would discover a new enthusiasm for social studies if you were," she heard herself saying.

He grimaced. "Thanks for adding cradle-robbing to my sins."

His self-deprecation made her guard drop even more. "You wouldn't have to rob a thing. By fifth period girls would be dropping into your arms like flies."

"Great, just what I wanted to hear—that I'd be a real heartthrob for the teeny-bopper set." He frowned, was quiet for a moment. "What are your kids like?"

She was startled by the question. What did he care what kind of students she had? She almost gave him a noncommittal answer and then reconsidered. It was a safe topic. "They come in all shapes and sizes and degrees of talent and need."

"Need?"

"Yes, need," she repeated thoughtfully. "If they don't get adult attention at home, they crave it at school. And of course, they need to be accepted by their peers, to be one of the crowd. Junior high kids are restless, driven. My adviser in college used to tell me there are only two kinds of people in junior high, the quick and the dead. The kids are quick, and the teachers are dead—tired from trying to keep up with them."

He laughed, his Adam's apple moving in his darkly tanned throat. Then he controlled himself and said, "Check the bottom of this mess, will you? If we don't keep it even, we won't have a chance of getting the thing to stand up by itself."

She gave him the last one to hold, made a quick perusal of the stack, and walked to the table to pick up the rope.

He looked at her sleek body clad in the well-fitting jeans, the supple way she moved as she bent over the table, and said in a faintly smooth tone, "What about the boys? Don't they enjoy having a young, attractive, unattached woman teacher to look at every day?"

She turned to face him, her guard up, the liking she felt for him gone. "I don't know," she replied, her voice cool. "You'll have to ask them." She stood in front of him clutching the rope.

After the little beat of silence, he said, "Thread the rope through in front of me while I've got a good hold on the shock."

Every one of her senses clamored as she stepped in close, took an end of the rope, and nudged it between his waist and the stalks. The back of her hand registered the feel of smooth cotton over the hard flatness of his stomach. Warmed from his exertion, he exuded a faintly male smell that mingled with the dry leaves and tantalized her nose.

Her fingers were clumsy. At last, she got the rope around the stalks and pulled it tight. He came from behind the stack to help her, taking the rope to pull it taut while she tied the knot. When it was secure, he said, "How is this thing supposed to stand up?"

"You flare the bottoms like this." She leaned over and tugged at several, making them bow outward. The stack lurched crazily to one side. Ty caught it and gave her a bland look. "Got any other suggestions?"

"Hang on to it for a minute while I do the other side."

"Are you sure the Pilgrims went through all this?"

She smiled. "They didn't shock the corn, at least not the first year. They ate what the Indians gave them."

He looked down at the honey-blond of her hair, a flow of molten gold over the shoulder of the blue T-shirt she wore. The ends of satiny hair lay just above the jutting curves that pressed against the thin cotton. She seemed all of a piece with the earth colors of the corn shock they had made, all tones of cream and gold, her skin lightly tanned. What had she done this summer? Who had she spent her time with? That sweet-uncle type she was seeing? Something kicked deep in his stomach.

She finished tugging at the stalks. "Let go of it. I want to see if it will stand up."

He stepped back and thrust his hands in his pockets. The shock stayed upright, and she looked pleased. He said, "You need a few pumpkins scattered around."

A faint pink color tinged her cheeks. What had he said to make her color up like that?

"I forgot to get them from Stan."

He kept his face noncommittal, trying to ignore the graceful way she came up from the floor with her back straight and her chin high. He remembered how that slim, womanly body had yielded against his for just a moment. . . . "Why did you forget them?"

Her eyes flickered away. "You—distracted me."

He tightened his muscles, forcing himself to maintain his lazy stance. He had sworn he wasn't going to scare her off this time. This time, he was going to let her set the pace. But his hands ached to touch her. He wanted to reach out and grab. But he couldn't; he knew that. She would hate him. He tried a delicate probe. "I could apologize for distracting you"—he saw the betraying flicker of her eyelashes, and steeled himself to go on—"but I'm not going to. I'm not sorry." He leaned back against a desk, but underneath he was taut as a string. "I'd like to disturb you a lot more—"

"Don't." Her voice came out low and husky.

He curbed his impatience. She had to be feeling something; he was experienced enough to know that. She was breathing faster than normal, and her cheeks were still pink, but she hadn't moved from where she stood—a foot in front of him, her rear pressed against the table. If he took a step forward and she didn't move, he could trap her there. . . .

He didn't want her that way. He wanted her to come freely into his arms, her face filled with joyous delight. Was that pure fantasy? It must be. But that image of her smiling, her eyes sparkling, spun inside his head like a looped film.

She gripped the table with her hands, and every part of her rational mind screamed to her to move, get out. But the other part of her, the part that longed for the brush of those long, lean fingers, the press of that well-shaped mouth on hers, whispered to her to stay—stay and find out what he was going to do. . . .

His face and his body were cool, unreadable. Then his low voice said softly, "You took a step toward the truth just now. Take another. Come here."

The soft promise of sensuality in his words made shivers prickle up and down her spine. "I—can't."

Not a muscle moved; not a eyelash flickered. "Why not?"

She turned away and walked to the window, stood there with her back to him, staring out at—what? What was she seeing? He'd bet it wasn't the school yard.

"There's—nothing left in me to give. I'm—empty."

The bleak words tore at his soul. If she had cried and screamed, she couldn't have affected him more. Those words told of grief and anguish and pain. . . . He went and stood behind her, his hands clenched at his sides, his gaze caressing that beautiful head. He ached to know what was going on underneath that heavy, silky hair. "Why are you empty?"

She whirled around. "Because—someone took it all away—" Her brows were squeezed together in anguish, her eyes tortured. He stared at her, wondering how much longer he could keep from pulling her into his arms. The room vibrated with a humming silence.

Afterwards, he couldn't have said whether she moved or he moved. It was a simultaneous coming together, a movement by two parts of one mind. His arms went around her and he pulled her close and stroked her back. "Leigh," he murmured huskily, "I'm very sorry—more sorry than I can say."

She shook her head and tensed her body, creating a space between them. "Why should you be? You don't even know me," she said, raising her head to look at him.

"Don't I?" he said softly, his voice huskily disturbed as he bent to let his lips brush hers. The words came into her mouth on his warm breath. "I know you. You've been inside my head, living with me for years. I just couldn't find you—"

He took her in his arms, and she was brought up against a strong, rock-hard body. A delicious sense of relief exploded inside her. Here was a man she could lean on, depend on—trust. She tilted her head to receive his kiss, savoring his warm protection. She had never felt such gentleness emanate from a man before, and she was drowning in it. Then, subtly, the tenderness changed and became passionate demand. His lips nudged hers, and as her mouth softened, his tongue slid inside. The warm, wet flesh caressed and probed in a moistly erotic dance. A driving urge to respond made her answer with provocative thrusts of her own. He moaned, a half-agonized, half-ecstatic moan. The soft male sound scaled her hidden barriers, and desire fountained upward. For a long, heady moment, she received all his lovely intimacies and returned them with a hungry eagerness . . . until his hand moved just under the curve of her rounded breast. At the touch of his fingers on her curved flesh, she shuddered and jerked her head back, breaking off the kiss and trying to thrust him away at the same moment.

She didn't succeed. His grip was unyielding. She was locked against him at waist and hips. For a long moment he held her in his firm grip, his blue eyes dark. Then his mouth quirked, regaining its normal, mocking slant. "And that from a lady who says she has nothing to give." The mobile mouth tilted into a half smile. "I think I found the—residue."

She put her palms against his chest to push him away, but on her first tentative push, his fingers tightened their grip on her hips, and the heat of his chest under her hands weakened her resolve. "Not enough to matter," she said coolly.

He gave her a long, considering look. "By whose standards? Yours—or mine?"

Memories came rushing in, and her blood cooled. "Let go of me," she said. Instantly, his hands fell away, but somehow she didn't feel the relief she should have felt. "This is a waste—of my time and yours," she said, trying to maintain control of her voice. He moved slightly, and she felt the leap of her pulses. *Oh God, I'm falling for this man, and there's nothing I can do. I've got to send him away.*

She braced herself, curling her fingers into her palm. "Let's—be honest with each other. You claim to—care how I feel, to want to know me, to feel sorry for me. Yet you're perfectly willing"—she hesitated, cleared her throat—"that is, if I read the signs right—" She faltered, looked at him, gathered herself to go on. Bluntness was always best. Bluntness turned any man off. "—to amuse yourself by taking me to bed for a one-night stand. Actually"—her voice remained steady, by what miracle she didn't know—"you don't give a damn about me."

He didn't move a muscle. "Taking you to bed wouldn't be amusing."

Stung, she cried, "What do you think it would be?"

He was cool, enigmatic. Then a shoulder lifted lazily. "I don't know. You are full of surprises. I'm—intrigued."

He lowered dark, sooty lashes to shield his eyes from her view. Her blood cooled, and even cooler reason returned. She must be out of her mind to stand in her own classroom talking about going to bed with a man she barely knew.

She made a graceful, outflung gesture with her hand. "Well, you'll just have to go on being intrigued. I'm not going to go to bed with you to satisfy your curiosity."

He let a beat of time go by. "You've already satisfied my curiosity." His gaze never wavered. "I had another more important . . . satisfaction in mind."

The sexual innuendo ignited a long-quiet nerve in the pit of her stomach. "Go to hell," she said, each word distinct.

He gave her a long, considering look. "I was right about you, wasn't I? You can love as passionately as you hate."

"What we exchanged wasn't love."

"No, it wasn't," he drawled, surprising her with his agreement, "but it was a damn good stand-in."

She gazed at him, her gray eyes smoky. "You're nothing but a cheap opportunist, a people-user."

He watched her, his face closed, blank, his arms folded against his chest. "Do you feel better now that you've lashed out at me?"

She reeled, stunned by his keen perception. He was too intelligent, too sensitive, too close to the truth. She couldn't breathe. She had to get out, away from him. "Just don't try to use me."

He stared at her. "You liked being in my arms as much as I liked having you there. But now you're frightened. Why, Leigh?"

"Get out." Her voice was low, tortured.

Whatever thoughts he was having were carefully hidden behind that hard face with its square chin. He examined her mercilessly for a moment longer and then turned and walked away, his back straight, his tall body a moving picture of lithe animal grace and male pride. She felt as if she had been stalked by a predator—and then released from its grasp. When she heard his step on the stair, her breath left her body in a long, sighing groan.

CHAPTER FIVE

Ty handled the Trans Am carefully, controlling his temper. The sun was low in the sky, and he drove against it, squinting. He had left his sunglasses in the apartment. Springwater was shadowy, still, with no one about. A gray cat ran out from between two buildings, headed on a collision course with the car. Ty swerved sharply. Cursing, he caught a glimpse of the animal teetering at the edge of the road, his front paws braced to counteract the momentum in his rear end, fur and hackles raised, green eyes wide with fear.

Like Leigh, he thought grimly.

The cat turned tail and ran, leaving him to resume his controlled speed and turn onto the street where Eve lived, thoughts of Leigh revolving inside his head like a carousel. Why had she responded to him and then turned him off cold? Why did he represent danger to her? Whatever it was, it was far beyond her fear of being interviewed. Fear on a deeper, more primitive level had made her break off that kiss and shove him away—and try to alienate him further with words.

His mouth tightened. Had she been raped? That didn't make any sense, either. If she had, she certainly wouldn't have allowed him to get close to her, much less exchange passionate kisses. Would she? *Would she?* God, he didn't know. Mentally, he went back over what he knew of her. Mother exploded on the screen with a hit movie in her early twenties, married the director, had Leigh. Trouble in the marriage. Director escaping into the wilderness to climb mountains, and to, as he told the press, renew his spirit. Killed in a fall from a mountain in Sierra Nevadas. Mother already involved with another man who would be the first in a long line of lovers. Leigh raised by hired help while living with her mother in Hollywood. At the age of fourteen, on a vacation in the Adirondacks where she had driven to keep an assignation with another man, her mother met and married Dean Masters. Marriage lasted six months. Claire left, Leigh stayed. Obvious affection between the stepfather and daughter—nothing there.

He turned into the driveway in front of Eve's house, his hands clenching the wheel. There had to be something.

What's the matter, Rundell? Can't stand the thought of a woman turning you down?

No, that wasn't it. If it were any other woman, he'd shrug his shoulders, pack his bags, and leave town without giving her another thought. But he'd been caught in her spell since the first moment he had seen her face in those pictures. . . .

It was true enough women had seldom said no to him, especially in the last three years since his films had been such big hits, but he took no pride in his success with women. They were, with few exceptions, predatory females who were interested in one thing—furthering their career. There had been minor variations on the theme—the smarter ones who'd refused and all the while given him signals they'd certainly reconsider if he offered them a part in one of his films, but there had only been one or two of them that had captured his interest for more than a month. The women he had met lately had a remarkable sameness about them, as if there was a factory somewhere in L.A. that was turning them out of a mold: blond hair, their mouths alive with a bright gaiety that didn't reach their eyes, their hands nervous, constantly them for what they were, an attempt to protect herself. He was a perceptive man, Mr. Ty Rundell, perceptive—and dangerous. Was it possible he knew about Paul? A sickness washed over her. No, he couldn't. Paul was on the East Coast now appearing in a play.

She threw the afghan back and walked quietly to the window to stare out into the gray light. Wisps of fog gathered over the creek. Across its narrow silver width, a weeping willow bent spidery branches earthward. She couldn't see them, but she could remember how the hollow branches broke off and fell to the ground around the tree. But the tree grew new ones and persevered. That was what she would do. She would throw off her memories—and she would persevere.

Deke sat back, watching the play of the lamplight on Eve's face. "Thank you for that meal. It was excellent."

Eve gave a faint laugh. "How excellent can sandwiches be?"

"Maybe it depends what you're comparing them to. I've been living on restaurant food for the past three weeks, and home-cooked chicken salad is a real treat."

As if his compliment disturbed her, she stood up quickly to carry the dishes away. He said, "Can I help?"

She shook her head. "There aren't that many, really."

He watched the graceful, quick movements she made as she picked up their plates and cups and walked around the curving snack bar where he sat to the dishwasher tucked under the counter.

She said, "How long have you known Ty?"

Deke thought about it. "We go back about fifteen years, I'd guess. I was an old hand in the stunt business, and he came on the lot like the young bucks do, wanting a job. I liked him. We made a few pictures together and discovered we hit it off. I knew he was a tiger, right from the first. When he'd learned all I could teach him, he started on the cameramen and techs. Pretty soon he knew more than I did about camera technique, lenses, set construction, and action shots. He wouldn't be the success he is today if he hadn't had such a thorough background in movie-making."

He watched the firm roundness of her hips press against the green silk as she bent over to put a plate in the dishwasher. Desire stirred, low and deep, with a strength he hadn't felt since Donna died. He got up from the snack bar and went around to lean against the curving arch of the entrance to the tiny kitchen. He had to be careful, very careful. Eve had dropped her guard when he'd told her about losing Donna, but he wasn't sure of her. One move toward her would make her back away. He'd been just about to kiss her when Ty had knocked on the door. He'd threaded his hands through her hair and was pulling her toward him, caressing her nape—and she wasn't resisting. His mouth had been inches from hers when the knock sounded. He'd had to stifle the urge to curse. . . .

She seemed to take a long time clearing away. Now she was wiping the cupboard with a terry towel. He stepped forward, said her name softly. "Eve."

She turned, her face flushed, her eyes brilliant. "Yes?"

He took a step, not exactly trapping her against the counter but taking advantage of the barrier to her retreat to pull her into his arms.

"Deke, please—"

He shook his head, breathed her name, and kissed her nose, her cheeks, the delicate skin at the temple where her pulse was flickering at a rapid rate.

"Deke, I—"

"Don't tell me to stop. Not now. Not when I've been wanting to do this all afternoon—" He smoothed a tendril back from her ear with fingers that shook, and it was that trembling touch with its vulnerability that undid her. She turned her mouth up to him. He took it gently, tentatively, as if she were a young girl receiving her first kiss.

Her hands, pressed flat against the denim of his shirt, made an involuntary movement. The pads of her fingers brushed the light covering of hair on his chest, and he reveled in that contact of flesh on flesh. Taking it for the encouragement he needed, he moved to tighten his grip on her hips—when suddenly, her whole body tensed and she pushed at him violently. He released her, but before she could move away, he reached around her and grasped the counter top, trapping her.

"What is it?" He gazed down at the top of her head, seeing the intricate whorls and mussed fullness of her dark hair and felt an overwhelming surge of tenderness.

"I'm forty-one years old," she said huskily, "too old to be taken in by your—Hollywood charm."

She lifted her head and gazed at him, her green eyes brilliant. He clamped down on his temper and met her gaze steadily. "And I'm forty-five years old—too damn old to be put off by name-calling."

She flushed and her eyes shimmered with temper. "I wasn't—"

"Sure you were," he said easily. "You gave me a label and you stuck it on my back and you're not about to look underneath it."

Her slim body with its mature curves tautened. "I don't have to look underneath. I know what I'd find."

Deke watched her, not missing a flicker of an eyelash, a movement of a muscle. Under the smooth skin at her throat, a pulse beat at an accelerated rate. He stood, his arms almost but not quite touching hers as he held her trapped. Underneath the green silk, her breasts pressed against the fabric. He'd gotten under her skin, and she didn't like it. She didn't like it at all.

He relaxed slightly, and Eve made a restless movement, as if she expected him to release her. He didn't. "I get the feeling," he drawled, "that you've been hurt—perhaps recently"—his eyes narrowed—"and in our age bracket I'd guess the damage was done by some guy who already had a wife."

She started with surprise, hot color sweeping up into her cheeks. "What happened in my life has nothing to do with you."

He contradicted her in his slow voice. "Right now"—he let his eyes travel slowly over her face and wander lower to where her shallow breathing was making the silk tauten across her feminine curves—"I'd say it did."

"You don't have any part of my life. You don't know anything about me—"

"It's the learning I'm interested in—" He moved to kiss her, but she raised her hands and stiffened her wrists, making a barrier between them. Her cool voice was at variance with her flushed face. "I've never liked one-night stands." She watched him, waiting.

"What makes you think that's what I want?"

She said, tilting her head, "You couldn't want much else, could you? Our life-styles are a million light-years apart—"

"I could want a lot more—" He leaned toward her again, but she pushed him away. "No, Deke. Don't. This is a road to nowhere, and I've been that route. I'm not taking the trip again."

"Tell me about it."

She shook her head. "No. I was a fool once; I won't be again."

He dropped his arms and straightened. He had lost this round—but the battle wasn't over. He wanted her—and somehow, her resistance fired his blood rather than cooled it. He knew why. Underneath her resistance lay that tantalizing response to him, a momentary softening of her body and sweet yielding of her mouth that made him want her all the more. He hadn't failed entirely; he knew that.

He leaned forward, and before she could move away, planted a quick, hard kiss on her lips. Then he walked out of the kitchen, striding to the couch to pick up his jacket. His back to her, he missed seeing the look of stunned surprise in her face.

When he had shrugged into his jacket, she came out of the kitchen, her face more composed. He said, "Thanks again for supper."

"You're welcome."

He stood looking at her, his brown eyes clear and steady. "Will I be seeing you soon?"

She hesitated. "It doesn't seem likely, does it?"

He kept his tone carefully expressionless. "I suppose it depends on when Ty gets the car fixed."

She matched his look with a straight one of her own. "I think it would be better if we didn't see each other again, Deke."

"Depends on what you mean by 'better.' Good-night, Eve." He strode to the door and went out, wishing he felt as cool as he sounded.

"Have a good time?" Ty's voice sounded faintly sardonic. There was only one light lit in the apartment, an old-fashioned floor lamp designed to look like a candelabra and Ty was sitting under it in the lounge chair, his long legs stretched out in front of him, a legal pad of yellow paper lying in his lap.

"She's an interesting woman," Deke said easily, thinking he hadn't seen Ty in a mood like this since the distribution of his last film hit a snag.

"Yeah. There's a lot of those around."

"What did you do this afternoon?"

"Shocked corn," Ty said dryly.

Deke's lips curved in a smile. "Didn't sow any wild oats while you were at it, did you?"

93

Ty gave him a sardonic look. "Spare me the rural humor."

Deke nodded toward the pad in Ty's hand. "How's it going?"

"It isn't." Ty threw the pad down, rose, and walked to the window. His lean body restless with tension, he gazed out at the squares of light that showed from Leigh's apartment.

Deke shed his jacket, sat down on the sofa, and eased his feet out of his boots. Ty turned to him, his face hard with decision. "If I can't get the car fixed tomorrow, I'm going to borrow Eve's and take you into the city. I want you to catch a plane back to L.A. and do some investigating for me."

Deke's stomach kicked in protest. He didn't want to go, not now.

"What's the big hurry?"

"I need some information."

"What's new?" Deke answered blandly. "Who do you want me to investigate?"

Ty's voice was cool. "Leigh Carlow."

Deke cocked an eyebrow and gave Ty a dryly quizzical look. "I thought you already did that groundwork."

"When I was in L.A., I concentrated on the relationship between her and her mother. Now I want to know about the men in her life. Was there one? If there was, who was he?"

From his comfortable position on the couch, Deke gazed at Ty lazily. "Is this for the book?"

Ty frowned, his dark brows pulling together. "No. She's out of the book."

"Since when?"

"Since—she refused to be interviewed."

"You've never let that stop you before."

Ty's mouth thinned. "There's a first time for everything."

94

"Looks like there is," Deke said softly. "Are you serious about her?"

Ty stared at him, raked a hand through his hair, pivoted to look out into the darkness. "No."

Deke said irritably, "You mean I'm flying across the country just to satisfy your prurient curiosity?"

Ty whirled around, his face dark. "That's not what it is."

"Then why don't you admit you're hooked?"

His face looked almost gray in the soft light. "Be reasonable, man. I've only known her two days."

"Sometimes that's all it takes," Deke said implacably.

Ty turned to look out the window again, tension evident in the set of his shoulders. To the taut back, Deke said lazily, "She left Hollywood when she was fourteen to live in the Adirondacks with her stepfather. She went to college in Oswego and got a job teaching here her first year and has been here ever since. Shouldn't you be looking for a man here—in New York State?"

Ty faced Deke and thrust his hand through his hair again. "I don't know. It just doesn't feel right. The answer has got to be out there. I keep grasping on the edges of something—" He turned again to stare moodily out into the darkness. Deke waited. He knew better than to interrupt Ty's train of thought.

Ty stood silent for another long moment, then suddenly he whipped around and strode over to his sheaf of papers. "Wait a minute, wait a minute. Somewhere in my notes I've got something. Where is that?" His lean hands shuffled through the sheets. He read and discarded rapidly. "Ah." Triumphant, he held up a single sheet. "Here it is. Leigh was in L.A. the summer she was twenty. She went back to see her mother just before Claire died. She stayed on after Claire's death for six weeks—almost too long to register for college that fall. She had to petition for late registration. I remembered thinking that was out of character somehow."

"Did she get back in school?"

"Yes. Her academic record was such that it was granted without question."

Deke rubbed his chin thoughtfully. "Six weeks, eh? Did she stay in Momma's mansion?"

"Yes, she did. There were things to clear up, of course, but not much. Her mother was deeply in debt, and the mansion had to be sold to pay off creditors. Leigh got nothing."

"Which made it more imperative than ever that she finish her education."

"Exactly." He shoved the papers back into their original place in the pile. "What I want to know is—why did she stay out west so long?"

"That's what I'm to find out, I take it."

"Yes. Find out who she saw, who she talked to. There must have been a maid, or a hairdresser, or somebody who was a regular in Claire's house who could tell you something."

"You don't want much, do you? That was seven years ago."

Ty stared at him. After a long moment of assessment, his mouth curved upward. "If I wanted something easy, I wouldn't send you."

"One of these days, Rundell," Deke said lazily, "that line isn't going to work."

Ty said, "You really don't want to go." Deke made no answer. Ty's keen blue eyes raked his tall form. "Got a little something going on the side, have you?"

Deke half closed his eyes and drawled softly, "Let's just say that it's been so long since I've seen something I want, I'm afraid I've forgotten how to go after it."

"It'll come back to you," Ty said dryly.

"I can't do much if I'm three thousand miles away."

"There are telephones," Ty reminded him. "Call her."

Two days later, Ty was just as unsympathetic. Tuesday morning he drove with Deke in the newly repaired car to the city airport and purchased Deke's ticket. Then, with a firm hand on the older man's elbow, he guided him into the line waiting to board. Suitcase in hand, Deke tried one last protest. "Look, is it really necessary—?"

"Call Eve every night or whenever you like," he said shortly. "Just get my job done. And call me the minute you find out anything."

"You paying the tab for all these calls?" Deke asked as he surrendered to inevitability and walked through the metal detector to the final boarding area.

"Don't I always?" Ty asked dryly.

At the door Deke turned back. "Be careful of that new brake line on the way back into Springwater." His eyes gleamed as he planted the final jab. "Don't get hung up on the curves."

"I'll try not to," Ty said, a slight smile lifting his lips, knowing Deke was really referring to Leigh's shapely form. "Thanks." Deke laughed at Ty's dry tone and pivoted to walk through the door that took him out to the plane.

At Springwater Consolidated School the halls reverberated with the sound of moving feet and chattering voices. Leigh breathed a sigh of relief that it was seventh period, her free hour of the day, and opened the door of the faculty room. She stepped in and pulled it closed, shutting the noise out, making the oval burnt-wood sign that said Decompression Chamber rattle. Eve, sitting at the table leafing through the daily newspaper, glanced up. Leigh got her mug, filled it with coffee, sat down across from her friend . . . and said the thing that had been on her mind all day. "Are you seeing Deke again tonight?" At the moment they were the only two occupants of the long, narrow table. Ben Harris lounged in his usual corner of the worn, yellow plaid couch, well out of earshot.

Eve shook her head, her eyes bright. "He left for L.A."

Leigh felt her stomach give an odd little twist. "You mean they're—gone?"

"Not they—he. Deke is flying out this morning. Ty isn't going with him. He still has some unfinished business here, Deke said."

An odd jangle of annoyance and relief sang through her. "When will Ty be leaving?"

"I really don't know." Eve glanced up at her through dark lashes. "Want me to ask Deke tonight when he calls?"

"No." The negative came out crisply. Aware of Eve's curious and faintly amused look, Leigh brought the heavy mug, its side initialed with a big L, up to her lips. "I mean—I don't care, really, I was just—curious." She sipped the hot liquid and then set the cup down carefully. "Deke is calling you tonight?"

Eve colored slightly and nodded.

Leigh's eyes were bright above her cup. "Do you like him?"

Eve gave an overly casual shrug. "What's not to like? He's an—interesting guy."

"I thought you were off men."

Eve shot her a straight look. "I thought you were, too."

"I've been seeing Hunt—"

"I said men, honey, not males who've never lived anywhere away from mother in all their forty-five years of life."

"Hunt has to take care of her—"

Eve gave a soft little grunt. "Since when does a barracuda need tender loving care? Hunt doesn't count and you know it and I know it. I think even Hunt knows it in his more lucid moments."

"He's good company."

Eve lifted a shoulder under the sleek dark purple sweater she wore. "It's a good thing you think so. He drives me bananas." Eve tilted her head to one side and gave Leigh a long, considering look. "Somehow," Eve said softly, "I can't imagine Ty Rundell jumping when his mother said 'jump.'"

Leigh couldn't either, but she retorted, "What has that got to do with anything?"

Leigh's eyes had gone silver, and that was a bad sign, but Eve pressed on. "He's interested in you, isn't he? And you're interested in him, too, at least you should be if you've got a brain in your head. Why don't you give the guy a chance? At least, get to know him a little."

"It's out of the question," Leigh said coolly.

"That all depends on what the question is," Eve shot back, getting up to rinse her cup and stash it back on the shelf above the sink. Before Leigh could reply to the gibe, she was gone.

Forty minutes later she walked to her classroom, telling herself that Eve was wrong. She couldn't let Ty Rundell get near her again. And she wouldn't. She would forget that surge of disappointment she had felt when she thought Ty had gone without even saying good-bye.

She went into her room and sat down at her desk, her eyes not focusing on anything. She was ready for her class. Her students would come in soon, stumbling, running, or walking decorously, depending on who was in charge of the legs and what mood their owner was in, and they would demand all her attention. But now the room was quiet, and her eyes drifted to the tall corn shock standing in the corner, just as Ty Rundell's throaty laugh seemed to echo in the silent room. *"I'm not your private scarecrow."* She closed her eyes. She could see him, his tall lean body covered with leaf and tassel bits, his face dark and casually mocking. But later, his eyes had gleamed with desire—

Out in the hall a bell rang, and a young girl swooped into the room and circled round Leigh's desk anxiously. "Miss Carlow, I don't have my paper with me. I left it in my locker. Can I go back and get it?"

She focused her eyes with difficulty. "Yes, Michelle, go ahead."

"Miss Carlow, I forgot what the assignment was. Can I do it and bring it to you in the morning?"

Leigh sighed. "No, Jennifer, the assignment is due today. You can do the extra credit assignment listed on the board to make up your grade, if you like."

Mark Farrish came in and sat down at his desk with a maturity and assurance far beyond his years, and Leigh was reminded once again of Ty. Where had he gone to school? If he lived on a ranch, he had probably ridden on a school bus to get there. What kind of teachers had he had? Had they recognized his quick intelligence, his drive to succeed, his facility with words? Her eyes drifted to the corn shock. She saw a body bent, shoulders pushing against the cotton fabric of a T-shirt, rounded buttocks and lean thighs straining denim . . . She blinked, shut out the image. She still hadn't gone to get the pumpkins. . . .

Driving back from the city, he saw them on the roadside stands, pumpkins perched like orange globes on the wooden stalls. He pulled off the road and bought several: three large, two medium-sized, and four smaller ones. He gave the surprised young girl a generous tip and carefully carried them three at a time to the trunk of his car, whistling.

That evening Leigh sat in the house that was too quiet, the drop lamp in the kitchen shining down on her honey-blond hair. With a resolute determination, she kept her eyes on the papers in front of her, touching her pencil to each answer in an effort not to miss one. But her mind kept wandering away. Ty had returned to the apartment, she knew, because his car had been parked on the street in front of the house when she came home from school.

She hadn't seen him since that disastrous Sunday. Would he try to see her again? Or had he written her off? She didn't want to see him. "I don't," she mumbled aloud with a fierce intensity—and knew she was lying to herself.

She shoved the papers aside and tossed the pencil down on top of them. "You can't run away from it," Dean's voice echoed in her ear. "You've got to learn to deal with it. Don't hate yourself for what your mother was. You're only responsible for you."

A longing to hear Dean's voice sent her to the phone that sat on the table by the couch. She put her hand on the receiver—and pulled it away. She had made a vow that she would not call Dean just because she needed him. She called only when she had good news; a student had begun to improve, or she'd read a new book she liked. She hadn't even called him the night there had been an old movie of her mother's on television.... She'd sat there and watched it, commercials and all. She'd forced herself to remember—and to try to forgive. She wasn't at all sure she'd succeeded.

A knock sounded on her door. She froze. There was a moment of silence, and then the knock went again.

He stood out in the hall, wearing the same jeans he'd worn that Sunday afternoon. His denim shirt was a slightly darker blue, the cuffs rolled back. In his hands, propped against his chest, was an idiotically small pumpkin.

He said, "Happy Halloween." Then, quickly, before she could answer, he handed it to her. "A peace offering."

"Thank you," she said, in that low husky voice that seemed to be very familiar yet shook him with surprise every time he heard it. The timbre was exactly like Claire's.

He leaned against the doorframe. "You're welcome."

"I—" She seemed very nervous. He wondered why. "Come in, won't you?"

His blue eyes flickered over her face. "Thank you, I will, just for a moment."

She had been working on papers, he saw, for only the drop lamp in the kitchen was lit, its pool of light falling on the scattered pile on the table. With a quick grace, she walked to the lamp beside the couch and bent to turn it on.

"Don't bother," he said softly. "I won't be staying long. I only came to give you the pumpkin—and to tell you that there are several more in various shapes and sizes waiting to be delivered to your classroom whenever you say."

She stood there, awareness of his attraction pulsing through her, wishing he weren't who he was, wishing she had the courage to ask him to stay for a cup of coffee. Her thoughts about Dean had weakened her resolve not to give Ty any encouragement. She knew her apartment would be bleakly empty when he walked out the door. "That's not necessary," she protested, her mind not on her words. "I can take them with me tomorrow—"

He shook his head. "Would I be interrupting if I brought them to the school around ten o'clock tomorrow morning?"

"Ten thirty is the break between classes," she said, setting the small pumpkin down on the table at the edge of the couch.

The look he gave her was bland, unreadable. "Ten thirty, it is, then." He turned to go.

CHAPTER SIX

He was almost out the door. She said quickly, "Would—would you like a cup of coffee?"

He turned, his face not quite as cool as it had been a moment ago. He was surprised, she could see that, and he wasn't trying to hide it.

"I only came to bring you the pumpkin," he said softly.

She recoiled as if he had hit her. "Yes, of course," she said stiffly and turned her back to him, wrapping her arms around her middle, feeling suddenly chilled and cold and wishing that he would go.

She heard the door close—and gasped with surprise when he caught her arms and pulled her toward him. For a moment he simply held her there, her back against his chest. His closeness made her quiver. He uttered a low sound in his throat and turned her in his arms. "You little fool," he said, holding her away to look into her face "I only meant I didn't use the pumpkin as an excuse for a reason to stay—" His hands moved over her back, their touch gentle and comforting, his eyes caressing her face. Then his pupils flared, become dark and enlarged, and the grip on her back tightened. "At least I told myself I didn't."

He lowered his head. His warm tenderness tore away the last shred of resistance. She raised her lips to his eagerly, all thought, all hesitation vanishing. A rush of elation filled her, sweeping her reluctance away. She wanted him. Her mouth and body clamored to know him completely. She wanted him to kiss her, touch her, love her. . . .

He sensed her changed mood instantly. With a naturalness that soothed, he urged her lips apart and thrust his tongue past the barrier of her teeth to explore the warm dark cavern that waited for him. She raised her hand in an instinctive need to touch him. The feel of the smooth cotton shirt and the hard flesh underneath encouraged her to slide her fingers upward under the material and find the well-shaped bones and muscles and to explore them with the palms of her hands. Touching his bare skin was an absorbing pleasure that, mingled with the probing of his tongue inside her mouth, sent tremors of desire spiraling up through her.

He held her closer, gliding a hand under her nape and threading his fingers up through her hair, the other hand clamped on her hip, making her acutely aware of his arousal. She should have fought off the waves of sensual pleasure that washed over her, but she couldn't. She gloried in the press of his hard body against hers, his chest crushing her breasts, his hips cradled in hers. He kissed her possessively, as if she were his and he were hers, as if their mouths had met long ago and knew all there was to know about pleasing each other. She was melting, sliding into a languorous need to have him go on kissing her forever, when his mouth left hers to wander down the sensitive cord of her throat and nestle moistly in the hollow, moving against her skin with the lightness of thistledown. "Leigh. My God. You're in my bloodstream—and I can't get you out—"

She was the one who was absorbing him, taking him into her mind and heart. "Ty—" He kissed his name from her lips, his mouth capturing hers again, tenderly rediscovering its full curves. He savored her with each touch of his hands. She was drowning and soaring at the same time, glimpsing heaven as she never had before.

His mouth fastened on hers, and he moved with her, taking her around the couch and down with him into its soft cushions, his hands gentle but insistent. She made a small sound of protest, and he feathered his lips across to her earlobe, nibbling it in consoling yet possessive love bites. "Do you know what those cries are doing to me? I want to kiss them from your mouth," he murmured against her lips, "and turn them into cries of delight—" He pressed her backwards until she half lay underneath him, his chest crushing her breasts. His eyes gleaming, he trailed a fingertip down the smooth skin just below her throat. His fingers trembled with a controlled passion, a passion that woke every cell in her body to vibrating life. Watching her, he let his fingers trail lower to the top button of her blouse. Deftly, he freed it. The brush of his fingers on her naked skin filled her with a sense of rightness that she had never felt with any man before. She breathed in sharply. He paused. "Leigh?" he said huskily.

"Oh, please—" Her husky groan told him she wasn't protesting. A smile curved his lips. He bent over her to nibble at the silken skin of her throat as he undid the next button, his fingers brushing over the front clip of her bra. He let his hand linger there for a tantalizing moment. She closed her eyes, waiting, her breath caught deep in her lungs. In an agony of suspense, she felt his fingertip move over the clip—and leave it intact to wander further down. She opened her eyes, long lashes fluttering back. His face loomed above her, lean and sensual, a faint smile playing around his lips. Another button was undone, and with a quick, practiced movement he pulled her blouse free. Cool air touched her skin—and brought with it a measure of sanity. "Ty—"

"Shh—" He covered her mouth with his own, his chest pressed against her naked midriff. Her whole body responded to him, her mouth softening to accommodate his, her hands reaching for the dark hair at his nape, her breasts still bound in sheer, satin-striped nylon nudging his chest, their buds taut in anticipation. He trailed his mouth down over her cheek, lower still over her throat, and lower still to the mature curve above her bra, the moist path of his lips an erotic promise of more to come. Keeping that promise, he tongued the deep valley, then trailed the moist, warm tip over her skin to send electric shivers chasing down her spine. Slowly, sensually, through the filmy wisp of material, he took the rosy center in his mouth and moistly teased the peak and circled its roundness.

She writhed with need and clasped his nape to urge him closer. He murmured against the soft skin of her breast, his fingers at the clip, "Let me love you, Leigh. I need you—"

I need you. Memory crashed in, and devastation followed. She rocketed upward, catching him off guard. Scrambling to her feet, she stumbled away from the couch before he realized what had happened.

"What the hell—" He looked dazed. She faced him, holding the edges of her blouse together, her gray eyes molten. He lunged to his feet and headed toward her.

"Stay away from me," she said, fear and self-hatred trembling in her voice.

He halted as if stopped by a brick wall, but she could see the effort it took him to do it. He was like a lion trapped in an invisible cage. In spite of what she wanted to feel, a flicker of admiration shimmered through her at the strength of his control. Cords stood out on his neck; his hands were clenched at his sides. She said, "I want you to go."

He stared at her. "I don't believe that."

"You must," she retorted, her voice a tortured sound.

He continued to study her for a suspended moment in

time. Then his manner changed subtly, as if he had recovered from the initial shock of her rejection and was able to think logically. He gave her a cool, reasonable look. "Don't you think you owe me some kind of explanation?"

She said angrily, "I don't owe you anything. All I want is for you to leave."

Those cool blue eyes examined her for another long moment. Then purposefully, he turned—and went to stand in front of the slanted windows and gaze out into the darkness just as she had done a few hours before.

Incredulous, she stared at the lean strength of his back pulling the material of the denim shirt, the tousled attractiveness of the thick, dark hair, hair disheveled by her own fingers. . . .

"What do you think you are doing?" She was angry and glad of it. The anger took away the pain.

He didn't turn to look at her. To the darkness, he said, "I believe it's called passive resistance."

"Well, you can do your—resisting—somewhere else." The dark head didn't move, and the sight of him made something rise inside her throat—along with panic. "I want you out of here." The words which should have been forcible came out in a low, strangled tone.

Slowly, he swung around to her. "Do you?" An arched eyebrow made his sardonic disbelief clear.

Furious, she cried, "Don't you understand plain English?"

"I understand enough about people," he said, "to know they seldom say what they mean—especially if their emotions are involved."

"There aren't any emotions involved here," she said heatedly.

Slowly, he let his gaze rove over her disheveled hair, her heated cheeks, her hastily buttoned blouse. "You felt—nothing? It was simply a physical thing with you?"

"Yes," she said, thankful to have such an easy out. "Yes."

His gaze held hers. "We were just engaged in a means of mutual satisfaction, I take it."

"Of course," she said, feeling calmer.

"Then why," he said softly, with a faint touch of menace, "shouldn't we just go ahead and—satisfy ourselves?"

She remembered cartoons she had watched as a child where a rabbit drew a hole around the fox and the hole suddenly became real and the fox fell through. She knew how that fox felt. She was falling too, falling through the hole Ty Rundell had drawn around her. "I'm not interested in—simple satisfaction."

"You seemed willing enough a moment ago," he drawled slowly.

"I've changed my mind."

"A woman's prerogative," he murmured.

"Anybody's prerogative," she said angrily. "I'm not accustomed to jumping into bed with a man on the slightest provocation—"

"Judging by your current reaction," he interrupted smoothly, "I'd say you aren't accustomed to jumping into bed with a man at all."

Her eyes flashed. "That will make excellent copy for your book, won't it?" she said sardonically.

The tiny muscle on the side of his jaw moved as if he were clenching his teeth. Then he said blandly, "Do you really want me to leave?"

"I thought I'd made that very clear."

"Have dinner with me tomorrow night." His tone was cool, matter-of-fact. She stared at him, dumbfounded.

"Just say yes, thank you, quickly, before you lose your nerve."

"No," she said coldly.

He shrugged as if her answer had been exactly what he expected and moved to the couch. With slow, elaborate movements, he sat down, stretched his legs out, and put his head back.

"What do you think you are doing?"

"Getting comfortable," he said. "I have a feeling it's going to be a long night."

"Get out of here!"

He closed his eyes. "I will—as soon as you agree to go to dinner with me."

"I wouldn't go to hell with you."

"I should hope not," he murmured.

She took a step toward him, not knowing what she could do. He opened one eye and looked at her. "Are you going to try to throw me out bodily?" His voice softened. "Go ahead." He extended his hand toward her and smiled. "We both might enjoy that." The lilting, sensual challenge in his voice made her back away.

Thoroughly panicked, she tried for a reasonable approach. "You can't stay there all night. You'll be uncomfortable. . . ."

"I've slept on worse," he said, folded his arm into his other one over his chest and closed his eyes again.

She clenched her fists in silent fury, checkmated. She took a step forward, her temper nearly goading her into a physical confrontation. But cool reason intervened. She wouldn't have a chance against that lean strength, and she had even less against his hard determination. All right, he wanted to sleep on the couch—let him! Let him stay there and get cold and end up with a crick in his neck. What difference did it make to her? She turned and went into her bedroom—and realized there was no key for the lock in the door. The house was old, and there had never been a need to ask Viola for the key to her bedroom. Not only that, she usually left the door open. The room would be an icebox in the morning if she didn't allow the heat to circulate.

She stood in the middle of her bedroom, shivering,

hugging her arms around her. She wouldn't sleep a wink knowing he was out there, knowing he could walk into her bedroom any time he pleased—and knowing that if he did, she wouldn't have the strength to send him away a second time. It wasn't only the cold that made her teeth chatter. She had been aroused . . . aroused in a way that had only happened to her once before in her life. . . .

Resolutely, she turned and walked back out into the living room.

"What time tomorrow night?" she said to the dark head that lay back against the cushions with eyes closed.

"Seven?" He didn't bother to open his eyes.

"Seven is fine," she managed to choke out.

He rose easily, with a lithe awareness that told her he hadn't been as relaxed as she thought. With a quick sardonic bow, he said, "Thank you for your gracious acceptance. I'll be looking forward to our evening together."

He went out and closed the door, but his mocking voice and smile taunted her as she locked the door and walked slowly into the bedroom. She felt drained, defeated. Somehow his absence was not the relief she had expected it to be. She dared not ask herself why.

She didn't sleep well that night, and when she looked at herself in the mirror the next morning and saw the dark circles under her eyes, she knew she would have to use more makeup to cover them or everyone would know that she had had a restless night. She showered and dressed and did her hair, trying to keep thoughts and memories at bay, but it was only when she got to school and heard the usual shouts in the hall and scuffling feet on the stairs that heralded the start of another day that she began to feel at least partially normal.

After a couple of hours, she had almost forgotten her devastating confrontation with Ty Rundell. Teaching school took all her concentration, which was what had made it so attractive to her in the beginning, and she realized suddenly that she hadn't thought of him at all through the first half of the morning. With a lighter heart she greeted her A section seventh grade with a smile that reflected her easier state of mind. Suddenly, a stir went through the group. The girls dissolved into self-conscious giggles, and the boys seemed to be sitting up straighter. She studied them, wondering what had caused this new disturbance—when into her peripheral vision moved a tall, lean, dark male. Ty Rundell stood just inside the door, his arms wrapped around a large cardboard box piled high with pumpkins. He wore the expensive leather jacket with a black roll-neck sport shirt and jeans, and he was just as disturbing to her senses as he had been last night. His attraction was heightened by the rueful smile, visible over the top of the box, that lifted his well-shaped lips as he stood at the door and faced the room full of curious teenagers he had obviously not expected to see.

"Sorry," he said in a low tone to her. "I'm a little later than I planned to be. Where do you want these?"

She fought down the shock waves that vibrated through her, cleared her throat, and said, "On the table will be fine."

He strode across the room with a lithe ease and deposited the box in the place she had designated, and she could almost hear the feminine sighs of admiration. He turned, sketched a quick, just-right salute to the class, bringing smiles to the girls and sheepish grins to the boys. As he passed her desk, he said in the same low tone, "I'll see you this evening."

He left the room, but the murmuring rose behind his retreating back like the wake churning after a boat. She sat for a moment, trying to gather her stunned senses. His kisses and caresses last night had made her forget that he had promised to bring her the rest of the pumpkins this morning, and his appearance in a territory she had thought safe knocked her off-balance. She struggled to retain control, suddenly aware that if she didn't do something soon, her class would be totally "gone." She flattened her palms on the top of the desk, taking comfort from the solid wood underneath her hands, and pushed herself upright to walk to the window, aware that the class was instantly alert to any action of hers.

She let them wonder what she was going to say and do and said nothing, giving the class a moment to quiet down. The room stilled. Self-consciously, Laurie Horton pushed a notebook around on her desk, and Mark Farrish slouched down into his seat and stuck his long legs out into the aisle. She glanced out into the school yard—and saw the one thing she did not want to see—Ty Rundell striding around the back of his gray foreign car, opening the door, and sliding under the wheel. She shut her eyes and turned away, but not soon enough. He moved with an economy of motion that was a pleasure to the eye and somehow sent all the memories she had been fighting to contain surging to the surface. His lovemaking had been like that too, a graceful movement of hands and mouth.
. . .

She fought to halt the sudden shakiness that attacked her knees, steadied her hand against the sill, and focused her eyes on the class. "Who can tell me something about the daily life pattern of the Iroquois Indian?"

When the class was over, she breathed a sigh of relief—until Laurie, one of the more mature, attractive girls, stopped in front of her desk. "Who was that super-looking guy, Miss Carlow?"

Leigh hesitated and then said coolly, "His name is Ty Rundell."

"He's fantastic." The girl ran a fingernail around the edge of her spiral notebook. "Is he your boyfriend?"

"No," Leigh said firmly, "he is not my 'boyfriend.'" The word seemed ludicrous applied to Ty.

"Umm, he looks like a movie star." A faint smile

touched Laurie's lips, and her eyes had a dream-dazed look.

Leigh said crisply, "You'd better go to your next class, or you'll be caught in the hall without a late pass."

Laurie came out of her romantic haze and threw Leigh a sheepish look. "Yes, Miss Carlow."

At lunch time she sat at the opposite end of the table from Eve, not wanting to field her questions. And underneath the rest of the day ran a strong current of apprehension—and something else, something too nebulous, too new to identify. It was almost as if—for the first time in her life she was . . . looking forward to the evening.

When the last class of the day ended and the building quickly emptied, she spent a few minutes arranging the pumpkins around the foot of the corn shock. She stepped back to view the final results and was pleased with her efforts. Ty had chosen well.

Three hours later her nervous anticipation had risen to an intolerable level. After her shower and shampoo she changed clothes three times, her feminine instincts battling with her fear until at last she settled on one of her dressier school outfits, a cream-colored silk blouse, a softly gathered wool skirt in shades of gold and rust and brown, and a dark brown velvet blazer that contrasted with the honey color of her hair.

Her indecision and the extra care she lavished on her makeup made her late. When the knock sounded on the door, she was still in the bedroom, applying her lip gloss. She decided to finish rather than go to the door with one half of her mouth done. Her hand shook and slipped, sending a bit of red color below the curve of her lower lip. She swore softly under her breath, snatched a tissue, wiped the whole business off, and started over again. The knock sounded again, more loudly this time, its tattoo communicating an impatience.

She finished, threw down the sable brush, and ran out

of her bedroom. She opened the door—and nearly received the force of his clenched hand that had been raised to knock again. He jerked his arm back and stared at her.

"I almost hit you," he told her, frowning.

"I'm sorry. I was—running behind schedule."

He gazed at her from under dark lashes. "I thought you had lost your nerve."

Stung, because she hadn't once thought of backing out and wondered if he had been hoping she would, she said sharply, "Are you disappointed that I didn't?"

He clamped his lips together as if to stop words from coming out that he wanted to say and said tersely, "Get your coat."

They were in the car and driving up the hill when she said, "Where are we going?"

"To the city," he said coolly.

"But that's forty miles away. Surely you aren't going to drive that far for a meal."

He leaned back in the seat, holding the wheel with one arm, the other lying casually at his side on the divided seat between them. "Why not?"

She stared ahead into the pink twilight, her pulses quickening. Ty wore a dark gray wool suit that had been cut to fit the breadth of his shoulders, the lean taper of his waist. His hair had been brushed to a careless fullness around his head, and his jaw was smooth and exuded the tangy scent of his after-shave. It would be an evening of much longer duration than she had imagined. She sat up in the soft seat and pressed her hands together in her lap. She felt as if a cool, clean wind had blown through the car touching her skin with an excitement that made her nerves tingle and her body tauten. A wild recklessness surged through her, and with a sudden lunge she took the initiative. "Why didn't you go back to California with Deke?"

His sidelong glance was quick enough, startled enough, to give her satisfaction. "Anxious to get rid of me?"

"You say you're no longer interested in interviewing me. If that's true, there's no reason for you to stay in Springwater."

Ty was silent for a moment, his eyes on the road. Then he drawled, "I said I was no longer interested in interviewing you. I didn't say I was no longer interested in *you*."

His words hung in the air, the smoky darkness of his voice reminding her of the way he had held her, the kisses they had already shared. She fought the rush of blood to her cheeks and said in what she hoped was a cool tone, "There must be someone in Hollywood anxiously waiting for your return."

He arched an eyebrow. "A woman, you mean?"

"Of course that's what I mean."

His smile was a mocking lift of his lips. "Would it bother you if there was?"

She shot back hotly, "Don't be ridiculous."

His mouth tightened. "Yes, that was an absurd idea, wasn't it?" He turned his eyes back to the road and lifted his free arm to the steering wheel to wrap his fingers around it, as if he needed something to hold to keep his temper under control. She sat back, wishing she had never agreed to come out with him, knowing the entire evening was going to be a fiasco.

"No, Leigh, there's no one anxiously waiting for my return." He paused, and when she didn't reply he said, "You know how it is in this business—you work with a crew on a project, and you become close to a few people. You begin to know them well—too well, perhaps. The project ends. You vow you'll keep in touch. But you don't. You get busy with another project and you're scrambling to make it work and you concentrate on it twelve or thirteen hours a day. You fall into bed at night and try to forget the rest of the world exists, because you don't have the energy to think about anything else . . ." He trailed away, staring moodily into the darkness.

She listened, and she thought of Claire. Perhaps her mother hadn't hated her. Perhaps she had treated Leigh with indifference because her career took everything, all her time, her attention, her emotional energy.

When the long drive was over and they topped the rise of a hill, the city skyline loomed ahead of them, the black angular lines of one skyscraper silhouetted against the pink glow of the sky and towering over lower buildings.

"There is something rather awesome about seeing a city all at once, isn't there," he said softly, as if their harsh exchange of words those miles back had never happened. "I get the same feeling when I walk into the theater and see a film that I've been working on for two years." He stared ahead, a brooding look on his face. "Millions of little bits and pieces and angle shots and retakes—all combined into one superhuman project. If it works, it's unreal, a miracle, unbelievable." He was silent for a moment. Then he said, "That's what makes all those long hours and the sweat and the strain and the frustration worth it, I guess. The film—finished, up there, on the screen, playing in half a dozen major cities at the same time." He gave her a sidelong glance. "I suppose you think that's the ultimate in an ego trip."

"Not at all. Movies are an art of expression. Why shouldn't you take pride in your work?"

"Why didn't you ever—try acting?"

"If you've done any research on celebrity children at all, you should know that's a ridiculous question."

"Afraid you couldn't live up to your mother's standards?"

"There was no 'afraid' about it. I was told any number of times I didn't have my mother's looks or élan."

"And you accepted those opinions as the gospel truth," Ty said smoothly, turning off the thruway and guiding the car down the street toward the center of the city.

"No one ever told me any differently."

Ty lifted his eyes to a traffic light, watched it turn from amber to red, and thrust his foot down on the brake. "I didn't see your mother in person. But I've seen all her movies and stills." He pulled the car into a parking ramp, waited for the machine to disgorge its ticket. "I've never seen you on the screen," he drawled, "but right offhand I'd guess that your brand of subtle sensuality kept severely in check would come across in a much more exciting way than Claire's blatant sexuality."

As if he had not just dropped a depth charge on top of her head, he calmly parked the car under the concrete canopy and turned to look at her. She struggled to contain her anger, keeping it hidden behind her cool face.

He half turned in the seat, his eyes searching hers. "Well?"

"Well, what?" she asked huskily.

"I'm waiting for the explosion."

"What explosion?"

"The one that should come when I tell you you're more sexy than your mother ever was."

"You're lying," she said coldly.

"Want me to prove I'm not? Say the word and I'll set up a screen test for you."

A pigeon cooed, the low sound fluttering in the unseen feathered throat. The parking ramp was dimly lit, but even so, the shadowed strength of Ty's face as he sat turned toward her, every bit of his attention fastened on her, made her shiver with apprehension.

"No."

He shrugged and got out of the car, and quickly, before he could come around to help her, she opened her door and climbed out.

"Suit yourself," he said softly, his face unreadable in the inadequate light. "Just thought I'd show you I was willing to go to the trouble to prove my point." He added, his voice soft, the hand he clamped on her arm hard as he escorted her into the elevator, "I was quite sure you wouldn't agree."

He said nothing more on the way down, leaving her to grapple with the fact that he had accurately predicted her reaction to his outrageous statement. She clenched her teeth together to keep them from chattering. He was close, insidiously close to the truth, and she stood beside him in the elevator, her stomach dropping from more than the action of the booth they were in. What a fool she was to come out with him. He didn't need to ask questions to find out about her life. All he had to do was probe delicately here and there. He was too astute, too intelligent, and too clearheaded to be brushed aside—and too devastingly attractive to be ignored.

She shivered when they stepped out of the elevator into the chilly, windy street, and he drew her closer to him, his firm grip on her arm turning her to her left. She tried to forget his onslaught on her senses and concentrate on the chill wind that met her full in the face. She knew where they were going. Tommy's Chop House was one of those places that tried very hard to sound and look inelegant. It was tucked in between a men's clothing shop and a small book store on Main Street, and the facade was so unpretentious that the uninitiated walked past without ever seeing it. But it was the "in" place to dine in town, both with the high-rise executives and the show business people. Dinner reservations had to be arranged far in advance. The food was astonishingly good.

Undeterred by the crowd standing in the entryway, Ty guided her through the crush of bodies to the maitre d', gave his name crisply, and was told his table would be ready in a matter of minutes.

"Care for a drink while we wait?"

She nodded and was taken by the arm to the narrow room off to the side where people, most of them men, stood or sat around a bar backed by an elegant stained-glass window done in clear blues, reds, and golds, its disjointed pieces making the composite picture of a Victorian maid playing the harp while her cat, sitting on a lush red velvet pillow, listened. Ty, by some mysterious process, found two seats near a minuscule round table and indicated she should sit down.

"What would you like? Something sweet with cream—a grasshopper or a pink squirrel, perhaps?"

"I'd like a vodka Collins," she said coolly.

For a moment she thought she had gotten under his skin. But his face was bland as he turned back to the bar to order their drinks.

In the semidarkness the only source of light was the window, but the bar area was hardly intimate. There seemed to be people layers deep everywhere she looked, and she nearly got her toes stepped on by someone standing just in front of her table. She pulled her feet in, crossed her legs, and tried to relax. One high-heeled sandal caught the pedestal support of the table and set it wobbling precariously on the thick carpet. She steadied it, thinking it wasn't any more stable than she was.

Ty, his dark head visible against the brightly colored window, turned away from the bar, drinks in his hands, and elbowed his way toward her. He handed her the taller of the two glasses, and she set it with its napkin wrap on the table. At the exact same moment, a man standing in front of them took a careless step backwards and sent the table tilting once again. Her drink slid to the floor.

"Watch it," Ty said sharply, straightening to confront the stranger, who was, by now, aware that he had done something wrong and was turning around.

"I'm sorry." Tall, thin, he seemed to have to look a long way to the unbroken glass and its spilled contents. "My God, did I do that? I'll buy you another. What was it?"

He was somewhere in his early thirties, Leigh guessed, and one of the artsy crowd. He wore jeans, a flamboyant red shirt, and a cowboy neckerchief. His high-heeled boots had nearly sent the table and Ty's drink flying when he turned around.

"Nate?" Ty's voice was questioning.

"Ty? Ty Rundell?" The younger man's face dissolved in relieved recognition. "What are you doing up here?"

"Working on a new project." Ty cast a mocking look over the other man's lanky length. "Didn't recognize you in costume."

Nate dropped his eyes to his own clothes and smiled sheepishly. "We're doing a promo for the play at Geva. How have you been, man?" Even in the dimness, he seemed alive with enthusiasm. "It's been ages." He looked down at Leigh with a pleasant glance, but once he saw her, his eyes lingered, taking in the smoothness of her cheeks, the soft fullness of her mouth. When he raised his eyes to Ty, they were admiring, envious. "Are you going to introduce me?"

"Leigh, this is Nate Gardner. Nate, Leigh Carlow."

The smile faded, was replaced with a touch of incredulity. "Leigh Carlow? Isn't your mother Claire Foster?"

"Yes." She had never denied the relationship, although she had wanted to many times.

He studied her for a moment and then said slowly, "That must be why you look so familiar to me." He shook his head. "No, that isn't it. I've seen you before, I know I have—"

She waited, breathing suddenly becoming difficult. "I don't think we've met—"

He wasn't deterred. "Wait a minute. I remember now. We were both—at a beach party at Paul Lange's. That's it."

The name seared her. "I'm sorry, I don't remember seeing you—"

"You went around with him for a while after your mother died, didn't you?" he said curiously. "He was an agent then, wasn't he? I remember hearing something about you going into show business." He gazed down at Leigh curiously. "Are you working as an actress?"

Ty watched her, feeling the tension in her body as if he were experiencing it in his own.

"No," she said in a strained voice.

Nate gave her a quizzical look. "You're not? I thought since you were with Ty—" He shrugged. "Paul's in New York City, did you know? Landed a plum role in *To Those We Love.*"

In the peculiar yellow light from the stained-glass window, her face looked ashen. "Yes, I—read about the play in the paper."

Inwardly, Ty cursed himself for choosing this place. He hadn't thought about seeing anyone he knew—who had known Leigh. Nate hadn't said much about her relationship with Lange, but he'd said enough. Ty could almost guess the rest. Here was the missing piece of the puzzle— almost. Nate had handed the information to him on a platter—and now, suddenly, he didn't want it. Nothing was worth watching her sit there and suffer like that. He knew Paul Lange. He was handsome and charming . . . and unscrupulous and manipulative.

Another, far more destructive thought occurred. Suppose she was still in love with him? The thought made him grit his teeth in anger. He had to get her out of here. "Why don't we just skip the rehash of old times, Nate, and you can order the lady that drink you owe her."

Nate's eyes moved back to Ty. He got a cool, undecipherable gaze in return, and with an almost imperceptible lift of his shoulders, he bowed to the inevitable. "Yeah, sure."

CHAPTER SEVEN

When Nate turned away, Ty said in a low voice, "Would you like to get out of here?"

"Yes," she said instantly, her eyes flashing a look of intense pain mixed with gratitude that went straight to a vital center deep inside him.

Out in the cool night air, she seemed to revive a little. He held her arm firmly, feeling the slender fragility of her bones underneath her coat. She was shaking, and it wasn't from the cold. He guided her into the parking ramp elevator, and when the doors closed, he fought the urge to take her in his arms. He wanted to protect her—take away that wounded look in her eyes. But his instinct warned him it was too soon. Not yet, not yet.

She let him put her in the car and sat huddled in the corner like a silent wraith, but when he started the car, drove out into the traffic, and took the entrance to the thruway, she took a long, shuddering breath and said, "Thank you."

"You're welcome," he said soberly, frowning at the road ahead.

The car sped on through the night. After another long silence, she said, "Nate will be left with an extra drink."

"He'll survive."

"I—suppose I owe you an explanation—"

"You don't owe me anything," he said roughly.

A feeling of relief and release burgeoned through her.

He wasn't going to probe and prod. "Thank you—again," she murmured.

He reached for her, his warm, masculine fingers clasping hers in an undemanding grasp. She gave him her hand willingly, knowing that his silent assurance was exactly what she needed at that moment. Tensile strength wrapped itself around her fingers, and warm human comfort flowed through their lean length. The sick wash of memories receded, and she put her head back and closed her eyes.

Still wrapped in a nebulous cloud of nonthought, she was aware of time passing, of headlights probing the darkness along the road they had recently traveled. But strangely, she felt no urgency, no need to escape. She was content to let the minutes tick by, content as long as she had that warm hand holding hers. . . .

When she had unlocked the door of her apartment, he raised the hand he had held for so long to his lips and kissed her fingers. Then, gently, easily, he moved his mouth across the short distance to her lips, and took them with a firm, masculine skill that was strangely undemanding. It was sweetly possessive, like a kiss following a night of love with its tender reminder of intimacies shared. When he lifted his mouth, she felt deprived.

That same gentle sureness in his hands, he grasped her shoulders and moved with her into her apartment. Drowsy with the warmth of the car and the drugging sensuality of the kiss he had given her, she made no protest. He closed the door and, then, slowly, he unbuttoned her coat, watching her as he dropped it on a chair. Unable to move, she felt his fingers traveling down her body, his knuckles brushing against the silk of her blouse. She murmured, "Ty—" Her velvet blazer went the same way as her coat.

Scooping her up in his arms, he carried her through to

her bedroom. "Ty—" she said again, into the warm and comfortable cloud that his arms wrapped around her. His name was a plea . . . and he knew it. He laid her down on the bed, his eyes brilliant in the soft light from the other room and followed her down, sitting beside her, his hip against hers. His eyes seemed to pin her to the bed, and his dark head and well-shaped lips were so close to her own they mesmerized her. She lay utterly still and waited.

For a long, silent moment he studied her, his face dark and sensual, a fingertip touching her kiss-softened mouth. Her lips moved to say the words that would send him away—when he closed the distance between them and brushed his mouth over hers with tantalizing feather lightness, murmuring her name. She lay quiescent, glorying in the undemanding caresses his mouth bestowed on hers. He asked nothing in return, and because he asked nothing, a wanton willingness to give him everything beat at the walls of her heart. With each drugging pass over her lips, he wove the silken cord of seduction more tightly around her. Her arms lifted, wrapped themselves around his neck. "Ty." She sighed his name into his mouth and he took her lips—more insistently this time.

"Leigh," he whispered. "Lovely Leigh. God, you're so soft and feminine." Silk slid, and cool fingers brushed her blouse aside. In the dim light, her skin gleamed through the filmy nylon of her bra. This time, Ty didn't hesitate. With a swift deftness, he undid the clip. Cool air feathered over her skin—and with it, the realization that for the first time in seven years she was glad to be a woman—for the gleam of pleasure that sparkled in Ty's blue eyes as the freed weight of her breasts nudged the material aside was decidedly masculine. Cupping her fullness with both hands, he worshipped her with his eyes, letting them rove over her creamy roundness and the burgundy peaks that were already taut with anticipation. A low muffled groan came from his throat, and he lowered his head. His silky hair brushed over her skin, making it tingle with delight. His lips trailed along one rounded curve, tantalizing her with light, teasing kisses that mocked her with their innocent feather touch—until he plundered deeper and deeper into the curving valley. "Ty—"

Her soft repeated moaning of his name made him laugh softly against her skin. His mouth discovered the full depth of the shadowed hollow and then wandered back up to the soft vulnerable place at her throat where the pulse beat. She felt each caress as if it were branded on her skin. He moved over a slow path of discovery, and he was going back—back to the taut peak that waited for his possession. Her breath was caught in her lungs as she waited. She moved restlessly on the bed, lifting her hands to his nape, threading her fingers through his dark hair, urging him on with her own caressing hands that moved down the corded strength of his neck and back.

"Patience, honey," he murmured against her skin. "We have all the time in the world—"

Cupping a breast with his hand, he sent his tongue on a sensuous discovery around her swelling curve, in one devastating circle after another, until she thought she would explode with ecstasy. Each circle impinged closer until, at last, when she was moaning with need, he captured the burgundy peak, the wet pointed warmth of his tongue circling, exploring, probing. She writhed in a superheated mingling of delight and agony, one last desperate attempt to regain her sanity escaping her lips. "No—"

He brought his mouth up to her lips and kissed the word away. "Yes, honey, yes. Let me love you. Oh, God, I want you so much—and you want me, you know you do. Undress me, Leigh. Let me feel your soft breasts against my skin—"

He took her fingers in his warm hand and urged them toward the buttons of his shirt. She undid the first one, faltering a little as the curling masculine hairs raked against her fingertips. The skin underneath radiated a heat that penetrated to her bones.

At the last button, the one just above his belt, she hesitated, her eyes lifting to his. He groaned, "My God, you know how to torture me, don't you?" He grasped the front edges of his shirt and ripped them apart, tearing the button away, pulling the ends of the shirt out from under his gray pants. He put his arms under her and brought her half-naked body up to his, his mouth coming down on hers hungrily. He was all demanding male, his warm hair-crisp flesh pressed against her breasts, his hand seeking and finding the sensitive hollow of her naked back. He was no longer tender, he was a passionate man determined to take possession of the woman in his arms—

And that's all she was to him, the woman in his arms—at the moment. The sensual haze, the dazed desire fell away. In its place came the sick knowledge that he had been kind and gentle for one reason—to take her to bed. She had weakened toward him—and now he was going to take her—just as Paul had. And after he made love to her, he would tell her coolly that he didn't love her—just as Paul had. And she would be as devastated as she had been seven years ago—or even more so. . . .

She flattened her palms against his chest and violently twisted her head to the side, wrenching herself away from him.

"What the—" He pulled away from her, his face dark and angry, as if she had slapped him.

"No, I can't . . . I . . ." A silence stretched between them. "Get out." Her voice seemed to come from a place deep within, a place that was numb with cold and fear.

"What is the matter with you?"

"Nothing is the matter with me." Except that I can't allow myself to be used again by a man, manipulated, hurt. Not even for the matchless pleasure it would be to make love to you, Ty Rundell, she wanted to say. "Nothing except that I want you out of my bedroom."

"Like hell you do!" He leaned forward to kiss her, and in desperation, she raised her hands and pushed at his shoulders, her nails digging into the firm flesh. He muttered an oath and caught her wrists, shackling them with his hands, thrusting them down against the side of her head and holding them there, forcing her to lie disarmed and helpless on the bed. "What is this," he growled, "some kind of sick game?"

Panic—and her own body's violent reaction to his hands on her wrists made her writhe and struggle to free herself. His grip was immovable, his fingers tensile living handcuffs. He merely held her, letting her exhaust herself, until at last she gave up and lay panting, her naked breasts heaving with her effort. "Let me go."

He stared at her, his eyes shimmering with fury. "No." The word was cold, flat.

"Can't you understand?" she cried.

"No," he said coolly, "I don't understand a damn thing. Explain it to me."

She turned her head into the pillow to avoid looking into those burning eyes. "I don't want you here," she said, forcing her voice to icy matter-of-factness. "This whole evening was a big mistake."

His voice crackled with anger. "My God, it must have been, you little tease. Do you get your kicks out of stunts like this?"

"No, no! Just because I exchanged a few kisses and caresses with you doesn't mean I want you to make love to me."

His eyes played over the creamy flesh still very much exposed to his gaze. He drawled sardonically, "I'd say we went far beyond 'a few kisses and caresses.'"

She struggled upward, catching him by surprise, succeeding in raising herself halfway off the bed. "I won't be—manipulated."

His hard hands pushed her down again. "Exactly how was I doing that?"

Her cheeks darkened. "Wouldn't you call seducing a woman you don't love manipulative?"

The answer came back sheathed in a quiet menace. "I don't recall your asking for an undying vow of devotion when I carried you in here. And you knew damn well what I had in mind—because it was exactly what you had on yours."

"That's not true," she said hotly. "I—responded because you—you were kind to me and I forgot about your predatory instincts. . . ."

"*My* predatory instincts?" The words lashed over her like a whip as he gazed at her from under hooded lashes. "What am I preying on? That icy little container that passes for a heart inside a woman's body?" A growl of disgust came from deep in his throat. "If that's what I'm after, I'm a damn fool." He paused, his eyes never leaving hers. "Something happened to you tonight. I offered you comfort—and you took it." His eyes narrowed. "I got very close to that guarded heart of yours, didn't I? You haven't been given much tenderness from a man, have you? Was your stepfather the only man who's ever been kind to you?"

"That's none of your business."

"It's becoming more my business minute by minute," he said heavily, sounding furious about it.

"No one asked you to get involved with me," she said hotly, his obvious regret making her emotions swirl around in a strange mixture inside her.

"You're right," he said. "No one asked me to do anything. I volunteered. But now I'm in this up to my neck. And if you could be honest with yourself for two seconds, you'd admit that you are, too."

"No," she said coolly.

He gazed at her for a long, tense moment. He was thinking; she could see that. That keen mind was turning over with the rapidity of a computer. Then, surprisingly, he lifted his hands and sat back slightly on the bed. "All right," he said, his voice soft and tinged with mockery. "What happens from here?"

His change of mood and tactic threw her off-balance. "I—don't know what you mean."

"You decide on the action and tell me what to do. If you say go—I go."

She opened her mouth, but before she could speak, he warned her, "But just remember it had better be what you really want."

"I've already told you I want you to leave—"

"You didn't mean it."

"I told you to go—"

"Tell me again." The words were clipped, cool. "But just remember, if you do—I won't be back. My system can only stand so much of your brand of stop-and-go loving."

She stood, looking at him, his lean length lazily at ease, in sharp contrast to the tense, angry man she had glimpsed a moment ago. How could he be so blasé if he really cared what decision she made? If she told him to go, he would feel a mild annoyance perhaps, nothing more.

"The truth," he said in a soft lethal voice.

The silence seemed to grow and build. At last, she said huskily, "Please, just—go."

His face hardened into something almost inhuman. If there was an emotion behind it, it was hidden under that tanned facial mask. The dark head bowed briefly. "For a moment there, I thought you were going to opt for the truth." He got up from the bed, his eyes playing over her still-bare curves. His mouth twisted. "Good-bye, Leigh."

When the door closed behind him, she felt an intolerable wrenching pain. It was beyond tears. She rolled over and buried her face in her pillow, wondering if the pain of making love to him and losing him would be as soul-destroying as never knowing his total possession. . . .

The phone was ringing when he opened the door.

When he answered with a short, sharp hello, Deke said in a puzzled tone, "Ty? Are you okay?"

"Yeah."

"I got the info you wanted. Paul Lange."

"Yeah, I know," he said shortly.

There was a little silence. "You do? Did Leigh—"

"No," he said shortly.

"Oh." Deke's tone indicated a hasty withdrawal from the sensitive subject. "Well, anyway, when Claire was in the hospital—"

"Skip it," Ty ordered roughly.

Another silence followed his crisp command. "You mean you—don't want to know?"

"You got it," Ty shot back.

"Are you still—"

"I'm not still—anything. I'll be packing up and heading out tomorrow. Look for me in four or five days."

His response was the puzzled silence that hummed on the line.

"I'll be in touch," Ty said, and rang off, knowing he had no right to vent his temper on Deke, and knowing that's what would happen if he stayed on the line. He lowered the receiver and stood by the couch for a moment, feeling blitzed. Deke's call confirmed what Ty had known instinctively after Nate had dropped Lange's name tonight and gotten such a violent reaction from Leigh. She had been involved with Paul Lange.

He strode to the couch and flung himself down on the cushions. His thoughts were so disjointed he didn't seem to have a logical thought left in his head. He clenched his fists. If he ever caught Lange alone, he'd strangle him. The man had obviously been Leigh's lover, and he'd hurt her, hurt her so badly she couldn't trust another man. Lange had had it all, her love and her body and he'd thrown it away.... Ty stopped in mid-thought, his mouth twisting in pain. Maybe it wasn't lack of trust that kept her from giving herself to him. Maybe she still loved the swine, loved him so much she couldn't bear the thought of being with another man.... His thoughts collided in his head. My God, he was jealous. Jealous of a lover she'd had years ago.... She was deeper under his skin than even he had dreamed, so deep he'd never get her out.... A low growl of disgust rose from his throat. He got up and prowled the room restlessly, feeling more caged and frustrated than he could ever remember feeling in his life. She was upstairs, lying in her bed, and one flight of stairs would take him to her . . . and God, he still wanted her, even if she was in love with another man. But he couldn't go to her and force himself on her. He'd given her the choice. He'd asked her what she wanted, and he'd held himself in an iron grip, not wanting to betray his own gut-wrenching anxiety, wanting her to make the decision on her own without any thought of his reaction. He'd prayed silently that she'd want him enough to ask him to stay....

He threw himself down in the nearest chair, knowing full well there would be no sleeping that night, knowing that the only way to preserve his sanity was to pack and get out of Springwater the first thing in the morning and put as much distance between himself and Leigh Carlow as possible.

She lay awake most of the night, thinking. She knew that Ty was at least partially justified in his anger. He was an adult male, and she was woman enough to know that any female who tried to play the tease with a man of Ty's virility and maturity was asking for trouble. She hadn't meant to tease him. She had simply let herself get lost in the warmth and tenderness of his caresses. She had wanted that—but it wasn't that simple. She had given herself in love once before—and—she shuddered. Could she forget those moments in the early morning hours when she had at last given herself up to Paul's kisses and caresses? Could she force those memories to the bottom of her mind and take the physical reassurance that Ty offered?

No, not without love. And yet. . . . She rolled over on her back and closed her fist in a tight ball against her stomach. She could still feel the warmth of his hand on hers, the understanding in his eyes. He had guessed she had been involved with Lange—and he'd still wanted her. Did that mean something? Oh, if only it did! If only he felt something for her. She might learn to love again. . . . She would see him tomorrow. She would see him tomorrow, and she would talk to him.

In the morning she had just reached the bottom step and was ready to open the oval glass door when she heard his quick tread on the stairs behind her. She turned to see his dark head lowered as he came downstairs, his lean body clad in the leather jacket and soft wool pants, the beige suitcase dangling from one hand.

She had no control over the words that bubbled up out of her throat. "You're leaving?"

His eyes mocked her concern. "There doesn't seem to be much reason for me to stay, does there?" he countered.

She didn't have any answer to that. The silence in the hallway reverberated with tension. She had to say something, anything to delay him a few more moments. "Have a safe trip."

He whirled back to her as if her words had struck him. "Damn you," he got out between clenched teeth. "Don't stand there and murmur polite little platitudes. Let the truth come out of that cool mouth for once. Say good-bye and good riddance and you're glad to see the back of me."

He turned away and missed seeing the shocked look on

her face. With unnecessary force he yanked the door open and walked through it, unaware that she was seeing his violent reaction with a newer, clearer vision. Her desperate words had made him violently angry, and that didn't make any sense—unless—he wasn't any happier to be going than she was to see him go. A shaft of sunlight streaked across the jet darkness of his hair. "Ty—"

He didn't hear her. He closed the door and strode down the steps. She stood for a moment, reeling from the force of his anger. He walked down the sidewalk with that lithe arrogant stride and levered himself into the car. Nausea climbed her throat and clung. She pulled the door open and called his name, half running down the steps—but he had already started the engine, and the car roared away, the dark head facing forward, never once tilting to look in the rearview mirror.

Five days later, on a Saturday afternoon, Eve sat across the table from Leigh and lifted a coffee cup to her lips, covertly studying her friend's pale face. She took a sip of the hot liquid, set the cup down, opened her mouth to say something, and closed it, telling herself it was none of her business—then heard herself saying, "Don't you think it's about time you told me what happened?"

"Nothing happened," Leigh said huskily.

Eve dropped her eyes and ran a fingertip around the rim of her cup. "You expect me to believe that?"

Leigh lifted her head. "Yes, of course."

"Well, I don't."

Leigh moved restlessly in her chair. Eve watched her with a silent compassion. How was it possible such a change could occur in five days? Leigh looked pale—if Eve wasn't mistaken, she had lost a pound or two off that already slim frame. Leigh put her cup down and made an expressive gesture with her hand. "Of course, why shouldn't you?"

"Because you're walking around looking like a ghost without a costume, and it's still three days before Halloween," Eve said dryly.

Leigh's shoulder moved. "Maybe I have a touch of the flu."

Eve made a little hissing noise with her mouth that was her favorite sign of derision and said, "Sure."

Restlessly, Leigh put her coffee cup down and got up and went to the window. Eve's house overlooked a different portion of the creek, but the view was just as beautiful. Three red maples on the other side of the tiny stream had turned crimson, their flaming color a brilliant contrast to the surrounding green of the lawn. "What do you hear from Deke?"

Eve hesitated for a moment and then said, "Not much. Mostly that he's worried about Ty."

Leigh's back stiffened, but she didn't turn from the window. "Worried about—Ty?" She did turn to face Eve then, and with the light from the window silhouetting her face, she looked even more like a dark wraith.

Eve nodded. "He hasn't arrived in California—and Deke hasn't heard from him since the night before he left." She was sorry she had told her. Leigh looked—devastated. But it was important that she know the truth. She might know something about Ty's whereabouts.

"There must be—some explanation," Leigh husked.

"Maybe there is," Eve agreed, "but right now, Deke is very concerned. He's going to wait another twenty-four hours—but after tomorrow, he's going to call the highway patrol." Eve looked down at her cup, then up into Leigh's stricken face. "You wouldn't have any idea where he might be, would you? Viola said she heard you talking to him in the hallway before he left—'driving the car like a bat out of you-know-where'—Viola's words, not mine."

Leigh managed a faint smile. "I did see him. We said—good-bye, that was all. He didn't say anything about

134

where he was going. I—just—assumed he was going back to California."

"Was he—disturbed about—leaving?"

Leigh turned to gaze out the window again, her back to Eve. "He was—angry with me over something I'd said. But"— she clutched at a straw, unable to even contemplate the idea that Ty might be injured or—dead—"he's an excellent driver. I'm sure he wouldn't have an accident."

"Even excellent drivers have accidents, honey."

"Ty wouldn't," she said firmly.

Eve pushed her cup back and lifted her chin to meet Leigh's intense gaze. "I hope you're right."

I have to be, Leigh told herself later in her room as she prepared for bed, stripping off her jeans and T-shirt. I have to be right. Even though he could never be hers, he had to be alive and well somewhere in the world.

But as she lay in bed and closed her eyes, images flashed in her brain, images of Ty trapped inside twisted gray metal hidden at the bottom of a ravine while cars passed unseeing on the highway above.

Time and again she woke, turning inside sheets dampened with her own perspiration. Her body was warm with misery, her skin alive with nerve endings that cried out in need. She needed the reassurance that Ty was alive. She needed to know that the warm male strength of him had not been extinguished.

Dawn arrived at last, and when the pale light filtered in her bedroom window, she knew she had reached a decision. She could no longer sit and wait like an obedient child for information about Ty. She threw the covers back and headed for the bathroom.

The dark blue teacher's key to *Our Larger World,* the textbook itself, and her lesson plans spread on the kitchen table in front of her, she wrote furiously, filling out the sketchy notes that would have been comprehensible only to her. Betty would need more detailed instructions in order to conduct the classes properly. The church bell rang, its deep resonant tone reminding her that she would be missed that morning. Her pen moved on over the page, not missing a word. It couldn't be helped. She would call both Eve and Hunt before she left.

A half hour later, she threw down her pen and scanned what she had written. Satisfied that Betty would be able to interpret her hurried scrawl, she shoved the papers inside the black plan book and rose from the chair. She needed a cup of coffee. She filled the coffee maker, flicked on the red button, and went inside to pack.

Her heart pounding, she told herself she wouldn't need much and threw a pair of pants and a pair of jeans in the suitcase that lay open on her bed. Two blouses and a heavy sweater were stripped off their hangers, and her nightgown and underthings followed the silky tops into her case. She would go in the denim pants she had on, and sneakers.

She closed the lid and carried the case with her out into the living room. The glowing red light on the coffee maker reminded her that she had forgotten to flip the switch to amber for the warmer. She did that and reached for a cup. Maybe she should take a thermos of coffee in case she decided to drive longer the first day. It was late already, and she still had to call Hunt, but she wouldn't be able to reach him until church was over. Curbing her impatience, she sat down to drink her coffee and wait.

The clock seemed to have stopped. The hands crawled around with amazing slowness and at last came to their nearly straight-up position that indicated it was eleven o'clock. She thought about going to the churchyard and catching Hunt outside—and discarded the idea. Her presence in informal clothes would arouse too much speculation—and when her decision to make this trip was known, that would be material enough for gossip without a beginning incident to trigger the townspeople's curiosity.

She got to her feet and carried her coffee cup to the sink, knowing that she couldn't eat a thing. Maybe she would be hungry later. She could stop and get something on the road. She had enough money to see her through for at least a week—but surely she would find out something before then.... At exactly ten after eleven, a soft knock sounded at her door.

"Hi." Eve stood in the hallway, a slightly worried frown creasing her brows. "I came to see if you were all right."

"I'm fine," Leigh assured her and stepped back to allow Eve entrance into the room. "Has Hunt left the church grounds yet?"

Eve cast a worried glance over her and then caught sight of the suitcase. "Why? Are you going somewhere?"

"I'm going out to look for Ty."

Eve stared at her, shock widening her eyes. "You can't be serious."

"I was just waiting to tell Hunt before I leave."

"You're out of your mind," Eve said bluntly. "How do you expect to find him on two thousand miles of thruway?"

"I don't know. I only know I can't sit around here and wonder if he's—" She made a choked sound and turned away to bury her face in her hands.

Eve's dress rustled softly as she stepped to Leigh to comfort her with a soft hand cupping her shoulder. "Honey, I had no idea you—cared so much."

Leigh lifted her head and shook it wordlessly, her face bleak.

"Honey, listen to reason. You can't go driving off down the road looking for him. You'll never find him...."

Leigh shook her head. "I can't stay here."

"Let me call Deke this morning," Eve said impulsively. "Ty might have arrived late last night—and you'd be going on a wild-goose chase."

"Use my phone," Leigh told her, gesturing toward the table at the end of the couch and moving to stand tensely by the window to wait.

Five minutes later when Eve put the phone down, Leigh turned to face her. "He's not there, is he?"

Eve shook her head, her eyes worried. "No. Deke is going to call the highway patrol in California. With Ty traveling interstate, he's not sure what they can do, if anything, but at least they can be on the lookout for the car."

The clichéd knock sounded on the door. Torn between her impatience to be gone and her relief that she would not have to wait for Hunt any longer, Leigh crossed the room and opened the door. Hunt stepped inside, eyed her informal clothes, and said, "No one seemed to know why you weren't at church. Are you ill?" He peered at her, his scrutiny registering the shadows under her eyes. "You don't look particularly well."

"I'm fine," she said shortly. "Hunt, I'm going away for a few days. I've gone over my plans and rewritten them for Betty so that she can substitute for me. You can call her tonight so she'll be ready for the morning, and when you do, tell her she may be teaching most of the week."

"Most of the week!" Hunt's eyebrows flew up. "Where are you going?"

There was a silence in the apartment. Then she said coolly, "Ty Rundell is missing. I'm going to go look for him."

Hunt's face grew almost comical with amazement. "In God's name, why? You're not a missing persons bureau. Let the police handle it—"

She said firmly, "No. I've made up my mind and I'm going."

Hunt cast a despairing look at Eve, who simply shrugged her shoulders and rolled her eyes to the ceiling.

Not finding any help in that quarter, Hunt stepped forward and caught Leigh by the shoulders. "Darling, don't be ridiculous. This man's disappearance isn't your problem."

"I've got to find him." The words were flat, cold.

"But—but you can't drive all over the country looking for someone. It's a preposterous thing to do—"

She gave him a clear steady look. "Call Betty tonight."

He stared at her, his attention, for once, focused entirely on her. "Are you saying you care so little for my opinion that it makes no difference what I think?"

Leigh made a helpless outflung gesture with her hand. "You're a friend, Hunt, nothing more. We both knew that nothing would ever come of our relationship—"

"I had hoped—after mother—"

Leigh shook her head. "No. It just—isn't possible." She walked to the table, gathered up her books, and handed them to Hunt. He stared down at them for a moment—then took them from her hands and said, "I think you'll—regret this, Leigh."

"Perhaps I will," she said steadily.

"You won't change your mind?" He was wistful—almost like a small boy.

She shook her head. "No. I'm sorry. I—can't."

Hunt turned to go, and she moved to open the door for him. She hadn't closed it completely when he'd come in and now, as she stepped forward to push it wide, someone stepped out of the shadowy hallway into the room, a man, slightly built, with a feline grace and coal-black hair and sharp narrow features that betrayed a shrewdness of mind, a smile playing over his thin lips as he took in the stunned reaction of the three people watching him. Then he said, "Hello, Leigh. Surprised to see me?"

What little color there was in her face drained away. The man's name escaped Leigh's lips like a cry of pain. "Paul!"

CHAPTER EIGHT

An awkward silence followed Paul's entrance into the apartment. He looked at Hunt, dismissal in his cursory glance. His eyes went to Eve, seated on the couch. He made a long slow tour of her slender body dressed in the creamy dress and white shawl she had worn to church, and the approval in his dark brown eyes was there for her to see, a challenge thrown to her. Looking at Eve, he said to Leigh, "Aren't you going to introduce me to your friends?"

She stared at him, trying to salvage some semblance of sanity, her brain spinning with questions and memories and pain, her lips somehow forming the words of polite introduction to Eve and Hunt.

Paul Lange cast a look around her apartment, not bothering to use his acting ability to hide his bored distaste. A few graceful steps took him around the couch. He sat down on the cushion next to Eve. With a slight, almost imperceptible movement, she edged closer to the corner of the couch and then got to her feet. "I must be going," she said coolly.

"Don't go on my account," Paul said lazily, giving her the full effect of his practiced glance, one Leigh had seen him perform a hundred times before. It started on a woman's mouth, moved leisurely over her face, then dropped to breasts, waist, and hips. She knew it well; she remembered the first time she had burned under those experienced eyes. No one had ever looked at her like that before, and she had been too naive to realize that Paul's perusal was a practiced art. She wasn't used to seeing such blatant sexual invitation in a man's glance. When she went anywhere with her mother, she was invisible.... People looked at her and then glanced away in disinterest, their eyes returning to gaze in awe at the beautiful, familiar features of Claire Foster.

"I was just leaving anyway," Eve said bluntly, her tone barely acknowledging Paul's presence as she walked to the door, her eyes on Leigh. "Give me a call before you go, will you? And why don't you give Dean a call, too? Let him know where you're going. If he should call during the week and not get an answer—"

"Yes," Leigh agreed, "I'll do that." She closed the door behind Eve.

Hunt didn't follow Eve out. He maintained his ground, an unsure bull steadying himself on the shifting floor of a china shop. Paul had turned and was favoring him with an amused grin, and Hunt didn't like it. He returned Paul's silent laughter with a faint hint of hostility. "Are you acquainted with Leigh?"

Paul's mouth tilted upward in a smile that was produced artificially. "We're—old friends."

Hunt's eyes flashed a question to Leigh, a sort of I-want-to-do-something-for-you-but-I-don't-know-what-to-do look that Leigh found mildly exasperating. The look was familiar and the emotion equally so, and it had the effect of bringing her back to earth. Whatever Paul wanted, whatever he had to say, she was immune.

"Don't forget to call Betty," she reminded him, taking his arm and gently leading him to the door.

"But—"

"I'll be in touch with you as soon as I get back."

With a firm hand on his arm she pushed him across the threshold. Hunt went, visibly reluctant. She closed the door and stood with her hand on the knob, her back to Paul. When she turned, her face was composed. "How did you find me?" she said bluntly.

Paul's eyes flickered. "I've always known where you were."

"Have you?" She lifted her chin. "Why are you here now?"

He seemed unperturbed at the icy coolness of her voice. His lazy glance around the apartment came to rest on her suitcase standing beside the door. "Have I come at a bad time?"

"Yes," she said baldly.

He smiled, his amusement genuine. "Any time would have been bad, wouldn't it?"

"Yes," she said again, her eyes steady.

He met her gaze, and then something, some of his brazen assurance fell away. The smile disappeared and in its place his mouth sagged, his eyes drooped in fatigue. He looked every one of his forty-two years. "God, I haven't been to bed since the performance. Any chance I could have a cup of coffee before you throw me out on my ear?" He put his head back on the couch and closed his eyes.

She opened her mouth to emit an angry refusal—but nothing came out. She got a cup down from the cupboard, poured out the steamy brown liquid, and walked to the couch to set the cup on the low table in front of him.

At the sound of the small, but definitely hostile click of the cup against wood, he opened his eyes and reached for it.

She said, "I want to know why you're here."

He cocked an eyebrow and set the cup down. "Old times' sake?"

She favored him with a stony, silent glance, and he made a pretense of cringing away from her. "You have changed, haven't you? What happened to that lovely child I once knew?"

"You happened."

He made another grimace, picked up the coffee cup. "And I thought it was those kids you've been seeing every day."

"What do you want, Paul?"

He set his cup down carefully on the table. "Why were you dining with Ty Rundell?"

"What?" Her cheeks reddened with anger. Nate Gardner must have rung him up. "What right do you have to ask that?"

The fatigue fell away, and in its place came the hard shrewdness, the feline cunning. He grasped her wrist. "Rumor has it he's doing research on you. He's in New York right now, nosing around, asking questions about me." His eyes were brilliant with anger. "What did you tell him?"

Ty was in New York! He wasn't trapped or injured or dead somewhere at the bottom of a ravine. He was alive. Relief flooded her in waves.

"Answer me!" Paul shook her wrist, his grip harsh and painful.

Her relief vanished, swept away by fury at Paul's rude grasping of her hand. "Let go."

"Not till you tell me—"

"I told him nothing—*nothing.*" Her face darkened and her voice trembled with fury. "Do you think I'd voluntarily admit to anyone what a stupid fool I was over you?"

His eyes moved over her face, saw the temper burning in her eyes. Her reaction seemed to reassure him. He relaxed and his grip on her arm loosened. "No, you wouldn't, would you?" His good humor restored, his lazy gaze moved over her. "Not now. Not the way you are now. You've changed."

"It's been seven years," she said icily. "Surely you didn't expect to walk in and find me exactly as you left me."

"I'm not sure what I expected," he said slowly. "Something a little more subdued, maybe. Nothing like what you are . . . fire under ice." He tilted his head slightly, his eyes assessing. "Actually, that total adoration you showered on me all those years ago was a bit wearing. I think I like you better this way, your body taut with angry dislike, your eyes sparkling. You're much more of a challenge."

Years ago, those words would have cut her to the quick. Now, they seemed to come from a distance, as if they were not even remotely connected with her. "I'm not interested in your opinions of me, Paul, not anymore."

"Seeing you like this," he went on in the same lazy tone, as if he hadn't heard her, "convinces me that I was right. You could have been a big star." His eyes narrowed slightly. "You've got what the public's looking for today, that sort of smoldering sensuality."

She stared at him, a faint sensation of nausea clogging her throat.

He went on, each word cool with self-assurance. "That fellow that was here—he doesn't look the type. Is he a good lover, Leigh?" He added softly, "As good as I was?"

"I'd like you to go."

"Would you?" He stood up and came to her. "Is that what you'd like? Or would you like to see if the old magic is still there?"

She stepped away from him, the tight control she had held on her temper gone. "There was no 'old magic,' " she said fiercely. "I was alone and lonely. I would have fallen into the arms of any man who looked at me without pretending I was Claire Foster. . . ."

"But I had an added fatal fascination, didn't I? I was the queen's consort," he said slowly, his voice soft and lethal, "and the queen was dying." He let the silence build around her. "Long live the queen," he said softly.

"I wanted your love," she cried. "I loved you—"

He shook his head slowly. "No, sweet. You didn't love

me. You might have convinced yourself that you did, but you didn't. You were using me to verify your existence."

"That's not true!"

His shoulders lifted. "It is, and we both know it. God knows it can't have been easy for you, living in your mother's shadow all those years. I didn't blame you. I even—enjoyed our little—rite of initiation. But I knew there could never be anything permanent between us." He gave her a sardonic smile. "You couldn't support me in the style to which I'd become accustomed."

"No, I couldn't, could I?" she shot back. "Not unless I did as you wanted and tried for a career in films with you as my agent. . . ."

Again that studied, elegant lift of the shoulders under the good wool. "I was giving you the facts of life, honey. I'm a man with expensive tastes. I was used to the good life your mother provided. Either you had to follow in her footsteps and try for the gold ring—or forget about me." An black eyebrow lifted in self-mockery. "You chose to forget."

"I'm not my mother," she said huskily.

"You couldn't have said that seven years ago. You were a mixed-up female then, wanting to be like her. But when I gave you the chance to compete with her on every level, not just a sexual one, you backed away like a frightened rabbit," he said softly. "The mere thought that you might actually be a better actress than she was filled you with terror, didn't it? You didn't want to be better, because if you were, she wouldn't love you at all, would she?" He paused and then added, each word distinct, "And you cared about her more than you did me, didn't you?"

Hot, angry color flooded more heavily into her cheeks. "There really isn't any answer to that, is there?"

Suddenly, Paul got to his feet. "I didn't come here to dig up the past and excoriate you with it. I only came to assure myself that you hadn't given Ty Rundell an unfavorable account of our time together."

With a sudden, clear insight, she said coolly, "Would an 'exposé' disturb the woman who's now keeping you in the style to which you're accustomed?"

He lifted his head, gave her a shrewd appraisal that contained a flicker of admiration. He hesitated, shrugged his shoulders. "Actually, yes. She's young—and she's not in show business. Her father made a killing in electronics and he's generous and so is she. I'm only working right now because she's abroad for a few weeks. But I know she wouldn't like it if my past love life were suddenly to appear on the supermarket bookracks."

"No doubt," she murmured. "Well, you can relax. There's no danger of that happening." Her words were crisp.

"Good," he said just as crisply, and went to the door. "I'll say good-bye, then. I've got to get back and try to get some rest before the show opens again on Tuesday." At the door, he turned, one hand on the edge. "Take care of yourself, Leigh."

"You, too," she said, the faint irony in her voice echoing in her ear.

She closed the door behind him, emptied his coffee cup in the sink, and went to the phone to call Eve and tell her that Ty was safe and alive, that Paul had seen him in New York City. Eve gasped with relief and rang off to call Deke at once. Leigh dialed Hunt's number, and when he answered, she told him in a cool, self-contained tone that he wouldn't need to call Betty after all, that she would be coming as usual on Monday morning. When he would have asked why, she cut him off. "I'll explain it all to you tomorrow." She replaced the receiver and carried her suitcase into the bedroom to unpack it.

Having Paul walk into her life again had been cathartic. She had loved him—and she had suffered the tortures of hell over the thought. But now, seeing their relationship from the vantage point of seven years, she realized suddenly that her love for Paul had been young, first love. It hadn't been the mature kind, the kind she would have risked anything for. Her feelings had all been mixed up with guilt and anguish she felt over her mother . . . who had died without ever really telling Leigh she loved her. Leigh had needed reassurance desperately, and she had turned to Paul. He had been older, sophisticated. She had been too upset and confused to see that her love for him wasn't real. It wasn't the kind of love that would make her pack her bag and get ready to drive over two thousand miles of thruway looking for one small gray car. . . .

She closed the suitcase with a snap and shoved it under her bed. She'd done the stupidest thing of all; she'd fallen for Ty Rundell.

She swore softly under her breath. Her confrontation with Paul seemed a minor irritation compared to that bit of unwelcome self-revelation. She went to the mirror, raked a hand through her hair. Why was Ty in New York? What possible reason could he have for making inquiries about Paul? Unless—she stood beside the bed, her heart pounding. Unless he was going to write about her after all.

Paul Lange pushed open the oval door of Viola Hendricks's old-fashioned house, and his eyes rebelled at the onslaught of bright light that hit him full in the face. Damn sun. He pushed himself out into the brilliant light and hurried down the steps, squinting, cursing himself for leaving his sunglasses on the dash of the car. A shadow loomed in front of him. Startled, he lifted his head and pulled back—just in time to avoid running into a dark, lean male.

"Hey," Paul cried in protest. "Watch where you're going!"

His upper arm was gripped in hard fingers. "What are you doing here?"

"What business is that of yours?" Paul peered into the face of his captor, a sense of self-preservation telling him not to do anything to antagonize this well-conditioned man who had grabbed his arm. "Who are you?"

"Rundell," came out from between gritted teeth.

It was just one more bad shock this fellow had dealt him, and in angry exasperation, he shook his arm. The hard fingers didn't loosen their grip. "Get off my back, Rundell."

"I asked you a question," Ty said coldly, standing in the other man's direct path to his car. "I want an answer."

Paul said a succinct word. Like lightning, Ty's face darkened and his grip ground against Paul's arm. "Answer me, damn you, or I'll rearrange that pretty face of yours."

"I've been talking to Leigh," Paul got out, his throat tight. In a spurt of defiance, he rasped, "Is there was a law against talking to people in this town?"

"What did you tell her?" Ty grated.

Paul Lange shot him another acid look. "I told her you'd been talking to people, asking questions about me. I wanted to know what she'd said to you."

"She didn't say a damn thing," he answered huskily. "She hasn't said one damn thing about you."

Paul Lange relaxed visibly. "She said she hadn't. I believed her. Hey, take your hands off the threads, will you?"

Slowly, with obvious reluctance, Ty loosened his grip. Paul stretched out his arm, brushed at the wrinkles Ty's hard grip had made in the dark blue cloth, his self-confidence returning. "You're pretty intense, you know that? You deserve her." He nodded his head up toward the top of the house. "You do have something going with Leigh, I take it?"

Ty's face was stony. "That's none of your business."

"Just like what happened between Leigh and me years ago is none of yours," Paul shot back, his face reddening. "Stop nosing around asking questions about me."

Ty gave him a contemptuous look through narrowed eyes. "What's the matter, Lange? Afraid your young, sweet little rich girl will dump you when she finds out what a long line of women preceded her?"

Paul stared at Ty Rundell, a cold fear touching his spine. If this man went to Janielle . . . "Just get out of my life, Rundell."

Ty said coolly, "All right. On one condition. You stay away from Leigh."

"Hey." Paul made a placating gesture with his hands spread outward. "She's ancient history."

"And you damn well better not come near her in the future."

Paul ducked his head in a mocking bow. "That will be my pleasure." He took a quick, wary side step around Ty, and with his shoulders set tensely, strode down the walk, his face burning. He owed Ty Rundell one. How could he get back at the arrogant bastard? Rundell was here in Springwater, and chances were good he was involved with Leigh. But he was a writer, a producer-director . . . and Leigh had hidden out in this little town for years because she was hypersensitive about her mother and the world of show business. Hadn't he heard something about Rundell researching the lives of children of celebrities? Chances are Rundell was playing both ends against the middle . . . telling Leigh he was in love with her while he gathered material for his book.

He thought rapidly. If he drove to the city and put in a call to Louise right away . . . Suddenly, he felt less tired. He got in the car and snatched up his sunglasses. He didn't need any more wrinkles around the eyes than he already had.

CHAPTER NINE

Knowing that every one of his resolves never to go near Leigh Carlow again had crumbled into dust, Ty Rundell stared up at the house. He'd known that five days ago when he'd driven to the thruway entrance and turned east instead of west and ended up checking into a hotel in New York City around midnight. He'd gotten a ticket for the play Lange was starring in and gone to the show the next evening. He knew one of the actors in the cast and he went backstage and asked some questions. He hadn't found out much about Leigh—but he had learned that Lange had been involved recently with a wealthy young woman from Long Island. He'd hung around for a few days, and then, knowing he was going to come back to Springwater, he'd checked out of his hotel and been on his way to see Lange after the performance last night when Lange got into his car and drove out of the city. Ty had followed him, curious. When it became evident what Lange's destination was, Ty had felt a surge of anger. Ty followed him to Leigh's door and then forced himself to wait outside. He'd watched Eve come out—then Hunt. He'd felt a touch of exasperation. Couldn't the man have stayed with her? But maybe Leigh had wanted to be alone with Lange. . . . He'd been relieved when Lange had come out a short time later, in less than twenty minutes.

He had to see her, talk to her, find out if she'd been devastated by Lange's brief visit. If she was in a state of shock . . . His mouth tightened, and he went to the trunk to lift out his suitcase.

She stared out the window at the creek, watching the way the sun glimmered off the silver ribbon of water and trying to fight down the restlessness. She knew she'd never be able to sit down and concentrate on that second stack of papers she had shoved into her book this morning. She might just as well admit defeat and . . . The knock on her door made her jump. The fear that Paul had returned for some obscure reason made her heart beat heavily in her throat as she walked to the door.

Ty Rundell stood on her doorstep in dark and disturbing full length, the male virility of him never more compelling than at this moment when his eyes burned over her.

He didn't move. His face cool, his blue eyes dark with a nameless emotion, he said quietly, "Hello, Leigh."

Seeing his dark, lean figure made a fireburst of joy explode inside her. After Paul, it was so good to know he was here, to know he had come back. The slight distance between them was intolerable. "Oh, Ty—"

She took two anxious steps forward and collided with him, throwing her arms around his waist and burying her cheek against his chest, her body needing to convince her mind with physical assurance that he was really there. Instantly, he folded her in his arms. "I hoped you might be glad to see me," he murmured, "but this surpasses my wildest dreams."

She breathed in the warm scent of him. "I thought I'd never see you again."

"Not a chance." He tucked a hand under her chin and lifted her face up to his. "Did you really think you could get rid of me that easily?"

She shook her head, tears gathering in the back of her eyes.

"You look thinner. What have you been doing to yourself? Have you eaten?" he probed gently, his eyes anything but gentle as they moved over her, studying every nuance of emotion in her face. He wasn't thinking of food. He was thinking what a fool he had been to believe she still loved Paul Lange—and what a fool he had been to leave her.

"I—no. Eve was here, and Hunt and—" She closed her mouth, and Ty's face darkened.

"I know Lange came to see you," he said bluntly. "I . . . ran into him outside."

"Did you?" she said steadily, her heart going like a trip-hammer, her eyes examining his face for a glimpse of his reaction. "He said you'd been asking questions about him."

She half expected him to deny it, but instead, he said softly, "I was."

She pushed away from him, her chin up, her mind remembering. "Did you find out what you wanted to know?"

"No."

"Why didn't you just ask me?" she said, her voice challenging.

"Would you have answered me if I had?"

She silently conceded the truth of that and turned away to block his dark and dear face from her sight. She didn't hear him move, but suddenly he was behind her, clasping her shoulders.

He gripped her, wishing he could wring the words out of her. He couldn't tell a damn thing from her reactions. She seemed just as she always had been, a woman inside a cage, a woman afraid to release the warm passionate part of her that lay hidden under that cool face. . . .

The warm strength of his hands on her forced her to mutter huskily, "You've decided to put me in your book after all."

Her words caught him unaware, made him grimace with angry pain, and involuntarily, his hands tightened on her shoulder bones. She winced, and at once he realized what he had done and loosened his grip on her slender body.

"I'm sorry," he muttered. "I just . . . Dammit, forget about the book, will you?"

"I can't," she whispered. "What other possible reason could you have for prying into my private life?"

There was a silence. "The best reason of all," he muttered.

She whirled around, her face pale. "Don't."

Driven by the unjustness of her accusation, he bombarded the cool wall of her face with words. "Don't what? Don't tell you that I can't get you out of my mind for a single moment? Don't say that everywhere I looked in New York you were there? Don't tell you that you've possessed me since the first moment I saw you?" He put his hands on her shoulders and drew her resisting body into her arms. His beautifully shaped mouth began a slow descent to hers. She trembled and made a move as if to escape.

"Don't stop me, Leigh"—his husky murmur vibrated through her body—"not now. Not when I need you so much. . . ."

She stared up at him, wordlessly watching his mouth come closer. The warm strength of him surrounded her and took away the cold, chilly loneliness she had felt ever since he went away. His palms on her T-shirted back warmed wherever they touched, and his hard muscled body took the weight of hers easily as she leaned against him.

"I don't want to stop you," she murmured.

"Thank God," he breathed passionately. "If you had, I'd have gone quietly out of my mind." His lips settled on hers with a tender possession that stirred her with its gentleness. He drew her into a marvelous world of sensuality with his mouth, stroking and nibbling at her lips, making her melt under his warm and tender onslaught.

Her hands found their way around his neck, and she pressed closer, basking in his tenderness as if he were the sun and she had been in the dark for a long, long time.

She felt him tremble. He lifted his head and pushed her away a hairsbreadth. His eyes dark with desire, he looked down into her face. She knew that it was all there for him to see, the love, the aching—the surrender. His pupils flared, but instead of kissing her again as she longed for him to do, he released her and took a half step away. "Let's get out of here. Is there someplace we can go? Are there any scenic spots around here?"

She stared at him, her mind reeling with the change of him. "Scenic spots?" she echoed stupidly.

"Anywhere," he said, his voice rough. "Because if we don't get out of here soon, I'm going to carry you into the bedroom and make love to you for the rest of the day and night—and I don't want to do that, not yet, not until we've talked."

"But I—"

A quick violent shake of his head stopped her words. "Think of someplace."

She tried to marshal her reeling brain. "Letchworth Park isn't too far."

"Letchworth Park?"

"The trees should be beautiful this time of year."

"Is it public?"

"Yes—"

"Then Letchworth Park it is. Get a jacket," he ordered roughly.

She hesitated for a moment and then turned away to do as he asked.

Inside her bedroom, her pulses still pounding with reaction to his kiss, she looked into the hinged mirror on her antique oak dresser. Below her flushed cheeks, her mouth pulsed with warmth. A sudden desire to look feminine made her rip off her T-shirt and tear a blouse from the closet. She put it on and turned to examine her image again. Her eyes were dark silvery pools, accented by the silky turquoise blouse. She opened the top drawer to find the triangular turquoise hair fastener Dean had given her for her sixteenth birthday. She bunched her hair at her nape and secured it with the clip. Tendrils escaped to curl around her ear, but she ignored them and turned away to pick up her sweater.

Ty's dark, sensuous face turned toward her as she reentered the room, and as his eyes moved over her, she felt that familiar little leap of pulse at knowing that her appearance both disturbed and pleased him. It was a silent communication between them, a recognition that he hungered for her. Yet he was holding himself back, giving her space and time and room, and because of his control, desire flooded every cell in her body. She averted her eyes to hide her aching need and said, "I'm ready."

He held out his hand, and she stepped to his side and took it, as if she had done that same thing many times before. His breathing was ragged as he tugged her out the door.

After he had slipped behind the wheel, she said, "I didn't bring any food—"

"We'll have something when we get back," he said easily, and set the car in motion. He drove through Springwater and guided the car up the long hill. She gave him directions, and the rural, rolling countryside passed leisurely by outside her window. Blue sky, brilliant sun, trees turning to flame. She had seen them all a million times. But today, with Ty, everything was new minted, glowing with color.

He glanced at her. "I can see why you like it here. It's like New England."

"I didn't really pick it for the countryside. Max told me

about the opening—and more or less put a good word in for me. He's Dean's cousin."

"Yes, I remember Dean saying something about a relative in the area—keeping an eye on you."

She smiled. "Max doesn't pry. He's too busy farming."

"A land lover," Ty murmured. "They're a die-hard breed."

"Like your father?" she asked, wanting to know about his family, wanting to know everything about him.

Ty shrugged. "He's the original man-of-the-land."

"Don't you miss Wyoming?"

"I try not to think about things I can't have," he said coolly, glancing at her, his meaning unmistakable.

She fought down the electric leap of her nerves at his cool glance and said, "You left Wyoming"—remembering what he had told her that first night they had gone for a walk in the chilly dawn—"because you couldn't be your own boss."

He was quiet for a moment, his hands steady on the wheel of the car. "I learned very early in life that the man with the money has control. What I didn't know then was that money talks everywhere, whether you're on a Wyoming ranch or a studio lot."

"So you decided to become a producer."

"Which even now doesn't give me the creative freedom I want. Production costs are so great that you've got to get several backers. And the more people involved, the more people there are to tinker with the story. Finally, so many people have had input that the original concept is diluted or lost along with the creative steam. Writing a screenplay by committee just doesn't work. But that's the way most of them are done, because in the last few years costs have skyrocketed."

"Your last three movies were successful."

"Only because I kept tight creative control by keeping the budget down, shooting on location, and working lots of odd jobs myself. Deke is a genius at figuring out ways to cut expenses. He earns his salary ten times over in a year."

"He doesn't look—shrewd." But she was remembering his smooth entrance into her apartment and the way he had successfully coaxed her into spending an evening with him.

"That's part of his charm. The local folk see me coming, and the price of food and shelter automatically goes up twenty percent. With Deke—" He shrugged. "Things stay reasonable. I've tried to analyze how he does it, but it eludes me."

They reached the entrance of the park, and Ty broke off speaking and thrust his hand in his pocket to bring out some money. After paying the fee, he said to her, "Any particular place you'd like to go, or shall we just drive until we see a spot to stop?"

"Just drive," she said. Her answer seemed to satisfy him. He lapsed into silence, slowing the car to accommodate the speed of the top-heavy recreational vehicle lumbering along on the narrow two-lane road ahead of them. The park teemed with cars. Many of them turned into the first area, where there was an olympic-size swimming pool, a snack bar, and a large restaurant. The pool was closed now, but cars were clustered around the other two buildings. She saw a family, a man and a wife and their two children, a boy and a girl, climb out under golden-leafed maples that shaded the grounds. The children scampered like young deer toward a rough wooden picnic table and swarmed over the top.

Ty drove on silently, following the road. When the car had climbed up to the top of the gorge, and the view out her window offered one particularly spectacular vista of rising slate-gray wall dotted with red and yellow maples, Ty pulled into the small parking area. He turned off the ignition and twisted to look at her. The intense glitter in his blue eyes made her reach out instinctively to him. "Ty—"

He made a sound low in his throat, brought her outstretched hand to his lips, and feathered his tongue over the sensitive skin of her palm. Her breath caught in her lungs. Abruptly, he released her hand and levered himself out of the car to come around and open her door for her. When she stepped out, he offered her his hand. She took it gratefully; her knees were wobbly and her senses still reeled.

He drew her forward toward the edge of the chasm. There, at a safe distance from the rim, they looked down into the four-hundred-foot-deep gorge that the ribbon of river had cut. The water was a pale green, and rocks lying in its path at a bend made ripples of froth spew out, drift downstream, and then disappear.

"I'm surprised they don't have railings along here," Ty said roughly.

"There are stone walls on the other side," she told him.

He stood looking out over the gorge for several minutes. Nothing in the way he held her hand gave her a clue to his thoughts. Then he turned to her and brought his other hand up to touch her cheek, cupping it in his palm. "That's what it's like for you, isn't it?"

She stared at him, her gray eyes brilliant. "What—what's like?"

"What making love is like. A deep chasm that you're afraid you'll fall into and never get out."

"No," she whispered, loving the feel of his fingers on her cheek, "not anymore. Not with you."

He made a low, rough sound, drew her into his arms, and said in a tone of wry self-mockery, "Now she tells me." He bent his head and brushed his lips over hers, kissing her with a gentle tenderness that was both tantalizing and devastating.

A low, appreciative whistle came from behind them. Ty

lifted his head, and from over his shoulder she saw the young man and woman, both in the standard college uniform of denims and T-shirt, standing a few feet behind them. The young man's face split into a sheepish grin before he grabbed the girl's hand and walked away.

"Whose idea was it to come to a public place?" Ty said huskily, keeping her firmly within his arms.

"Yours," she said, smiling up at him.

"I must have more rocks in my head than this place has," he chastised himself, "but there are still things that have to be said." He looked down at her, his eyes caressing her face. "I can rearrange my life to a certain extent. I can write anywhere. But there will still be things I have to do that you won't like. Attending movie premieres, for one thing, and giving an occasional interview to the press, for another."

"What does that have to do with me?"

"What does it have to do with you?" His grip tightened. "Dammit, it has everything to do with you. I want you in my life, Leigh. I want you with me. I want to roll over in bed at night and know that you are there. We belong together."

"You want me to give up my job . . . and go with you to Hollywood?"

"Yes," he said, his eyes never leaving her face.

She didn't move away from him, but he sensed her instant withdrawal and said quickly, "We don't have to live there. We can get a place further down the coast, or somewhere in the mountains if you like. But I do have to maintain contact with the film world."

She shook her head. "There's no place for me in that world. I don't belong."

"You do belong—with me," he said fiercely.

"No." She pushed at his chest. "I can't do it, Ty. Please don't ask me to."

He met her efforts to free herself with a stubborn resistance, but at last she tugged free and took a step away from him.

His eyes were like blue flames, touching her body with fire wherever they roamed. "You can't do it, Leigh." His voice held a curious flatness. "You can't walk out of my life."

"I must," she said.

He arched an eyebrow and said blandly, "A minute ago I got an entirely different impression."

"I'm sorry," she murmured, eaten with the knowledge that he could never be hers, that no dark-haired children looking like Ty would ever bound out of a bed and clamber over a breakfast table in her kitchen.

"A minute ago you told me you weren't afraid to make love with me."

"A minute ago you hadn't asked me to throw over my entire life."

His eyes glittered with a dangerous anger. "What were you going to do, have a quick one-night stand and then kiss me good-bye?"

"You make it sound so—so cheap—"

"Dammit, it is cheap!" He stared at her. "Once you called me a people user. What do you call what you were going to do?"

Unable to bear the anguished look on his face, she turned away. "I thought it was the sensible thing to do. It seemed to be the kindest way to—to say good-bye."

He made a half-strangled sound. She forced herself to meet his gaze. He stared at her for a long moment, and then took two steps away from her, as if he couldn't trust himself to stand too close to her. He stepped closer to the rim, facing it, his dark hair blowing around his head in the breeze that was stronger in the open. She caught back a cry of distress, her heart in her throat. "Don't go so close to the edge."

His dark face in profile was sardonic. "Don't bother to pretend you'd care if I fell down and bashed my head in."

Was it her imagination, or was he leaning out over thin air? Fighting to control her voice, she said, "Ty! Come away from there."

He was silent, staring out over the vista. Then he turned. A low and lethal voice from somewhere deep in his throat said, "Come and get me."

"Don't be melodramatic."

"I have a flair for the dramatic, remember?" He moved a half step that took him to the brink of the chasm, and her blood chilled in her veins. Like a panther purring, the words slid from his throat. "Come and get me, Leigh."

"You wouldn't—"

"You don't know that for a fact," he said coolly and edged closer until it seemed that the tips of his shoes no longer were touching the ground.

She cried out and reached for him, grabbing his arm and dragging him back with a strength born of fear and desperation. "You're insane," she rasped, the breath coming hard in her throat.

"I must be," he said huskily, folding her into his arms, "or I'd never have let you get this far under my skin. . . ." He took her mouth with a rough possession that stamped his claim of ownership on her. The young man who had whistled earlier gave out another piercing note, and the girl laughed.

Ty raised his head, his mouth twisted in a grimace. "Let's get out of here." He clasped her hand to haul her to the car.

He said little on the way back to Springwater, but once they had reached the house, he got out of the car and came around to her. As he took her elbow and began to guide her to the house, she said, "Ty, there's no need to prolong the agony. Let's say good-bye now."

He ignored her, pulled open the oval door, and shepherded her up the stairs. Outside her doorway he gave her a cool, assessing look. "You were willing to spend the night with me before I asked you to spend a lifetime with me. What's changed?"

"I can't. Not now."

"Open the door," he ordered her coolly.

"No—"

"*Open it.*"

His hard tone of command drove her to take the key from her purse. She unlocked the door, her heart drumming in her chest. "There's no reason for you to stay."

"There's an excellent reason," he said, following her inside and releasing the little catch spring so that they were locked in.

"I've changed my mind."

He shook his head. "Sorry. It's too late for that. What are we going to have for dinner?"

She stared at him. "How about a large order of reality?"

He shook his head. "Not my line of work. I deal in fantasies." He strode into the bedroom. She followed him, her cheeks red with color. "What do you think you are doing?"

"Setting the scene," he said coolly, taking the covers and ripping them back away from her pillows, exposing the length of soft blue sheets.

"Stop it!" She came at him, but the cool, emotionless glance he cast over her stopped her in her tracks.

"We'll have supper in bed. Let's plan something simple. We don't want to spend too much time in the kitchen. How are you at omelets?"

"Terrible," she said huskily, lying.

He lifted a shoulder. "I'll do it then. You can help."

"Ty, please don't do this."

He walked out of the bedroom and strode to the kitchenette. "I'll need a frypan, some butter, the eggs of course. Do you like tomatoes in your omelet?"

"No. Ty—"

"Good. We'll have tomatoes, then. Cheese. Do you have any cheese?"

"In the side drawer of the refrigerator. Ty, we can't . . ."

From across the tiny island of the snack bar, he raised his head and examined her with that dark, devastating gaze. "One night, Leigh. I want one night to remember. Are you going to deny me that?"

CHAPTER TEN

She stared back at him. How could she deny him when she ached for his possession? "The tomatoes are in the bottom drawer of the refrigerator," she said huskily.

He returned her gaze for a short, electric second. Then he smiled. "I'll need a sharp knife."

She came around the snack bar, opened the drawer next to the sink, and brought out a serrated knife and a small cutting board to lay on the counter top within his reach next to the stove. When she stepped closer to him, he caught her hand. She tried to tug it away, but he tightened his grip around her wrist and pulled her into his arms. Murmuring against her temple, he said softly, "Do you think I'm only going to make love to you when I get you in bed?" His breath was warm and caressive on her facial skin. "Our night starts now, here, while we're still together." He feathered a row of kisses down her cheek, over the top of her nose, and up along the middle of her forehead. She had no defense against his gentle caresses. She clung to him, savoring each kiss. His mouth wandered lower to the delicate lobe of her ear. He lipped its velvety tip lightly, with great care, his tongue coming out to moistly warm the hollow behind. It was an excruciatingly intimate possession, a tender taking of the secrets of the shell of her ear. She had never experienced anything like his gentle seduction, and she only knew she wanted him to go on learning all there was to learn about her until he discovered that ultimate of her secrets. . . . Her lips found the firm line of his jaw, and her tongue reached out and stroked the slightly prickly skin.

He gave an almost imperceptible shudder and lifted his head, his breathing unsteady. "The food, woman."

Heady with the power he had shown she had over him, she murmured, "Forget the food."

His grip tightened briefly. Then with a tempered strength, he pushed her away. "The food is part of the evening, honey. Now be good and get me that frypan."

She gave him a disappointed look, and he moved away with a visible reluctance and a taut jaw and took the eggs out of the refrigerator, put them in a bowl, and beat them up with what seemed to her unnecessary vigor, while she melted the butter in the pan. He reached across in front of her to pour the eggs in the pan, and daringly, driven by the thought that this night was all they would ever have, she slid her hands over the gauzy cream-colored shirt he wore, caressing his back.

Some of the eggs splashed down on the side of the burner. He said an explicit word and reached for a cloth.

"Am I bothering you?" she asked, all innocence.

"You've bothered me since the first moment I saw you," he muttered, wiping up the eggy spill.

She fingertipped down his back, enjoying the way his muscles moved under the cotton as he worked.

"I'm warning you, Leigh," he got out between clenched teeth, and she dropped her hand.

He turned and leaned back against the counter. "Did you know that's one of the things couples in sex therapy do because it's arousing—without being threatening?"

She shook her head. "No, I—didn't know. I only know I like to—touch you."

"And I like having you touch me," he said, his eyes dark. "Do you have the nerve to come here and take some of your own medicine?"

Her eyelashes flickered down. "I—don't know."

"Come here," he said softly.

Her body moved of its own accord.

"Lean against me," he instructed softly, bracing himself against the counter. "Let me feel the weight of your body against mine without my having to hold you."

She hesitated and then, driven by some mysterious inner force, she did as he instructed, feeling the hard muscles of his thighs, his taut stomach, his male arousal. Sensitive nerves in the deep well of her body quivered with awareness. His dark eyes flared as he felt the softness of her curved hips against his, but with a slow, controlled ease, he lifted the back of the silky blouse away from her pants. Carefully, right at the hypersensitive well of her spine, his fingers padded over her skin, moving with devastating slowness toward the nape of her neck.

She had never known just being touched could give such elemental pleasure. She pressed closer and circled his waist with her arms. Her head found a place in his shoulder that seemed to be meant for her. She was caught between a sense of contentment, and an aching that would only be appeased by Ty's possession. . . .

"I think the omelet is burning," he said softly.

"I don't care," she murmured. "Are you really hungry?"

"Yes," he rasped, "but not for food. Turn off the burner."

Reluctantly, she loosened her hold on him. Still in his arms, she reached around to turn off the burner and set the pan aside.

"Do I carry you to the bedroom, or do you walk?" he asked huskily.

"I'll walk." She smiled up at him. "You'd better save your strength."

He turned her against his hip with a half growl. "With you, that doesn't seem to be necessary." He clasped her around the waist and walked her across the length of the room, his voice husky with amusement. "With you, I seem to have more strength than I know what to do with."

At the sight of the bed he had readied, the sensual haze drained away. After tonight Ty would walk out of her life, and she would never see him again. She would be lonely, unbearably lonely, after having shared her bed with him. . . . She shivered, and he pulled her close. The warmth of his body and the touch of his hands swept away her thoughts of the future.

"Sit down on the bed," he said softly. "Not on the edge. Sit with your back against the headboard."

He knelt and removed her shoes. Taking her feet, he swung them up so that her legs were stretched out. Then, inexplicably, he pivoted and walked away, his tall male body disappearing into the other room.

She sat where he had left her, her mind unwilling to accept the fact that he had coolly walked away without saying a word. She heard cupboard doors opening. "What are you doing?" She swung her feet to the floor.

"Stay there," came the command. "I've found what I'm looking for."

He reappeared in the doorway, the cutting board she had laid out for him in his hand. A box of crackers and a round of cheese were balanced on top of it.

She watched him approach the bed, her eyes questioning.

"I told you food was part of the evening," he said huskily. "Usually lovers have days and years of sharing meals, but we only have tonight." He put the board in her lap. "I'll go back and get the wine."

It was all part of his slow, careful wooing, and a sharp ecstasy welled up inside her. He was taking great care to sweep away her fears, and she loved him for it. She loved him for this—and for a million other things. . . . He returned with a bottle of white wine she had forgotten she had tucked away in the refrigerator and one wineglass.

He filled the glass and handed it to her, his blue eyes gleaming with a brightness she knew was echoed in her own. She sipped the dry, tart liquid and handed the glass back to him. Watching her over the rim, he drank slowly.

His dark head bent as he set the glass down on the floor. He took up the cutting board to slice the cheese in wafer-thin slices, paired it with a cracker, and held it out to her. Automatically, she reached for it, but he shook his head. "No," he said, his eyes gleaming with bright challenge. "Show me that you trust me."

He held the tidbit to her mouth, and she ate it from his hand, her senses reeling with far more than the tangy taste of the cheese. His fingers were warm against her mouth, his hard hip nudged her thigh, and his eyes were drinking their fill of her.

"Your turn," he said softly.

She prepared a bit of food the way he had and offered it to him. He ate it and then kissed the fingertips that lingered on his mouth.

"Will you have some more?" he asked.

"I couldn't eat—another thing," she whispered.

"Somehow," he murmured, his eyes caressive, "I don't think I can, either."

He took the board and set it away. "I have a feast here in front of me," he muttered. "Oh, God, Leigh—" He leaned forward and gathered her into his arms, his mouth seeking and finding the soft, vulnerable hollow of her throat. His hands came up under her blouse, and the warmth of his palms against her back was electric, magnifying.

No longer able to tolerate the seeking caresses without an outlet for her love, she moaned and sought his mouth with her own. As if he understood her need, he lifted his head. She kissed him hungrily, urgently, her mouth opening to the pressure of his, her tongue stroking past his teeth, finding the wet moistness of his, teasing it with erotic, flickering caresses.

Their mouths still drinking from each other, he urged her down against the bed, pushing her just enough to clear the headboard. He half lay on top of her, his heavy weight against her breasts a delight. His hands traveled down the sides of her body, seeking out the feminine curves still clothed in silk and denim. She moaned and he lifted away slightly. "Am I hurting you?"

"Yes," she got out on an agonized sound. He frowned and pulled away, and she shook her head. "You're torturing me."

His frown disappeared and he laughed softly. "You deserve it. You and your fingertips started this, remember." He cupped her breasts, his thumbs finding their burgeoning tips even through her clothes.

"Ty—"

He shook his head. "You'll take your punishment, honey—for as long as I can hold out. . . ."

His hands continued their exploring path over her body, down the length of her denim-covered thighs, over her bare ankles to trace the sensitive bones of her arch. Sensual tingles radiated upward. She hadn't known such intense pleasure was possible from a gentle exploration of her toes. He retraced his path back up along the graceful lines of her legs, across her taut abdomen, up to the hollow of her throat. His mouth found the place where her vein pulsed close to the surface. She gasped in delight, and he chuckled low in his throat, a huskily disturbed sound of amusement. He raised his head, his smile fading. His fingers drifting to the button on her blouse, he scanned her face and asked the silent question.

In answer, she lifted his other hand to her mouth and sensually stroked the palm in moist circles with the tip of her tongue.

He groaned softly, his fingers moving deftly to loosen her buttons in four quick movements. Expertly lifting her out of the silky garment, he gazed at her, his eyes making her the feast he had called her a moment ago. Needing physical contact with him, she reached up to touch his mouth and trace the warm, well-shaped curves with a probing fingertip.

His fingers slipped under one strap of her bra and eased it down over her shoulder. He did the same with the other strap and then undid the front clip. Her bra followed her blouse, and the cool air filled her with a breathless waiting.

"Beautiful," he murmured, taking in the creamy perfection he had freed. "Soft and feminine and beautiful." He bent to her, his hair touching her skin. He feathered kisses over her, discovering the places where curve lifted away from bone, and then wandered lower to caress the underside of her breasts. She clutched his dark head, feeling the leap of her nerve ends everywhere his mouth touched. She threaded the vibrant silk of his hair through her fingers, her body aching for his mouth to ease the taut peaks that cried out for his possession. Against her skin he murmured, "Patience, honey. We have all night. . . ."

She made an agonized sound of protest, and his soft chuckle sent a shiver of anticipation and ecstasy over her skin. Then, as if he had at last taken pity on her, his warm mouth claimed the dark rose peak that waited for him. His tongue explored and teased, wooing one moment, possessively claiming the next. His mouth created torment and rapture, and in an agony of waiting, her body writhed with wanting.

His hands moved with sureness to the zip of her denims. He stripped them away, leaving her only in her bikinis. Coolly watching her, his fingers glided under the elastic. He slid the fragile silk down her thigh, caressing her every inch of the way, until the bikinis were tossed aside. His blue eyes roved over her nakedness and gleamed with a hunger that sent her already accelerated heartbeat pulsing at an even faster rate through her veins. "Now," he said softly. "Your turn."

She raised trembling hands to his shirt, aware in every fiber of her being of the taut masculine body under the gauzy material. It took endless seconds to free his buttons, but at last the task was done, and with his help, the shirt was tossed to the floor. She unbuckled his leather belt, undid the snap of his denims and ran the zipper down, her fingers drifting over his male arousal. A strange possessiveness seized her. For tonight, he was hers.... He stood up and unselfconsciously stepped out of his pants and briefs. She watched him unashamedly, taking pleasure in the revealing of his male beauty. His flanks were lean and trim, his waist narrow, the sparse dark hair that covered chest, thighs, and legs crisp and curly. He was a devastating male specimen with the well-proportioned lines of a Greek statue. But when he came down on the bed beside her, his breathing pattern disturbed, his hands seeking and finding the turquoise clip and freeing her hair to spill through his hands, she knew he was very much alive ... and that she had never been more so. He lowered his head and his tongue sought the slopes and valleys of a breast, its wet moistness making her tingle with delight. His path of discovery took him lower to her navel, where he tenderly and with great precision explored the tiny crevice. When she stifled a small cry of pleasure, his fingers smoothed over the flatness of her abdomen and the rounded curve of her thighs—and found the sensitive core of her desire.

Caught in a whirlwind of ecstasy, her hips moved, accommodating him. "Ty—"

He covered her mouth with a warm, possessive kiss, his hand still tormenting her with its gentle, intimate caressing. His tongue slid moistly into her mouth, dancing over her own. Then it was gone, its fire moving lower, seeking and finding her breast, circling the tautly dark center, making her body burn with need for him. His erotic onslaught on her mind and body and heart continued, sending her spiraling upward in desire. She cried, "Ty—oh, please—no more—I—"

As if he, too, could no longer tolerate the waiting, he moved over her and made her his, claiming her body in the final, intimate joining.

For a spine-tingling moment, he didn't move. She savored an incredible wholeness, a welding of the physical satisfaction and the overwhelming love she felt for him. It was as if everything she had ever been and ever hoped to be was centered in this moment of belonging to the man she loved. Then he began to move, making slow, circling drives against her, claiming her with his body and hands and mouth, taking her with him on a long, rhythmic journey of discovery that lifted her higher and higher into a rarefied world where only Ty . . . and rapture . . . existed.

He lay beside her, a finger tracing idly over her abdomen, his mouth touching her cheek. "Are you all right?"

"Yes," she whispered.

"No—ghosts?" The finger climbed the curve of her breast, wandered around its dark center.

She knew he was thinking of Paul. "No ghosts," she assured him. "From now on there will only be you . . . and the memories of this night. . . ."

He leaned forward and kissed her lightly, a gentle lover's kiss. "I'm glad. Are you sleepy?"

"A little," she admitted, not wanting to confess that his passionate lovemaking had made her lazily sated.

He reached down to pull the covers up over her. "Sleep, honey. We still have time. . . ."

He drew her against him, and she closed her eyes. After what seemed like a long, dreamless sleep, she woke to a room completely dark except for a sliver of moonlight streaming in the narrow window above her bed and light, teasing kisses caressing her face.

His voice close to her ear had a dark, husky sound. "Did I wake you?"

"Yes." She turned her head to better accommodate his searching mouth.

"Good."

He kissed her lazily in a smooth, undemanding claiming of her lips. She lay languid, relaxed under his mouth and hands, feeling his fingers glide over her like liquid silver as they took their pleasure in her curves and valleys. His intimate exploration wandered lower, grew bolder. She came awake, and her own hands found the well-muscled chest covered with crisp hair, the male nipples already taut, the flat stomach, the circle of his navel.

He made a muffled sound, and she drew her hand away.

"Leigh. I want your touch. I want you to hold me, touch me, know me . . ."

She renewed her caressing, wondering at her own temerity as she boldly explored his body, learning what pleased him by the quick, indrawn breaths he took. She leaned over him and kissed his chest, her long hair brushing his skin, her tongue seeking and caressing a male nipple.

With a stifled groan, he pulled her on top of him. At her small sound of protest, he cupped her breasts caressively, balancing her above him, his legs locking her against him. "Trust me," he whispered, his voice smoky, dark. "It will be good for you, I promise."

His thighs moved intimately between hers, and he claimed her once more. Deep within the nerve center of her body, she felt the intolerable tension build and build until that shuddering release rocked them both.

She slept again, and when she woke, pale streamers of dawn fanned through the window. A warm breath caressed her cheek, and hands clasped her naked waist while a gentle mouth took hers in a possessive kiss. Once again, his kiss was the prelude to a giving and taking of passionate delight that took her to the heights of heaven and beyond.

The alarm beeped its strident note. Her mind protesting the disturbance, she rolled over and reached for it—and discovered she couldn't. She was on the wrong side of the bed, and a warm, hard body lay between her and the clock. In a rush of sensation, it all came back; Ty's gentle, exquisite lovemaking, her own passionate response. Her blood raced warmly around her body—until she remembered that now it was over.

He stirred, lifted a dark-eyelashed lid. His gaze moved over her and there was tenderness in his eyes. "Good morning. What's that damn racket?"

"Alarm clock," she told him, nodding toward the stand on his side of the bed.

He reached out, fumbled, found the silencing button. "That's a god-awful sound." He raked a hand through his disheveled hair—and then he smiled—a dark, disturbing smile. "Are you the woman who kept waking me up and making love to me last night?"

His smile was contagious and her lips lifted. "Wasn't it the other way around?"

"Maybe it was," he admitted, stretching long arms up over his head and yawning. "Maybe I should try staying around another night, and you could have your revenge and—keep me awake."

The thought that he could speak so casually about what they had shared and could so carelessly consider staying racked her with pain. "I don't think that's a good idea," she said coolly, fighting to keep her voice steady. "We both knew you were going to leave this morning. Let's not prolong the agony." She made a move as if to throw the covers back, when he caught her arm. In one lithe move, he jerked her back and pinned her against the bed to lean over her. She stared up at him, fear and excitement clawing at her throat. He was blazingly angry; his eyes snapped with it. "Last night wasn't agony for you and you know it."

She wanted to cry out, *yes, yes, it was! Can't you see I can't bear to have you go?*

"No, of course not," she agreed in a cool voice that betrayed nothing of her inner turmoil. "It was very—pleasurable." *Dear God, what an inane word to describe what we shared!* "But now it's over. Isn't that the modern way? I get up and go to my job and you go to yours?"

His eyes glittered and his grip tightened in angry reaction. "You don't mean that."

Remembering that she was simply another woman he had taken to bed, she cried, "What's the matter? Aren't my reactions correct? Did you expect me to fall into your arms and tell you I'm madly in love with you?"

He gave her a sardonic smile, one dark eyebrow lifted. "Even I, as dramatic as I supposedly am, don't have the imagination for that."

Stung, she lay there, feeling raw and exposed. Did he believe her incapable of love? If only he knew how very much she did love him.... Her thoughts skidded to a halt. What would happen if he did know? What difference would it make to him? He had said he wanted her in his bed—but he hadn't said he loved her. And yet—

Taking every scrap of courage in her hands, she said haltingly, "Suppose—suppose we compromised. Suppose I flew out to you on weekends—or you came here when you could—"

His blue eyes pinned her to the bed. "Half a loaf?" There was a strange note in his voice, and a glitter in his eyes that looked like pain. He let go of her, twisted away, and sat up, presenting her with the broad, tanned surface of his back. "No, thanks. I've seen enough marriages fall apart under the strain of separation and the spotlight of the press to know that's not what I want."

"We weren't—talking about marriage."

"No," he agreed, standing up and walking around to the pile of clothes and sorting out those that belonged to him. "We weren't, were we?"

Slipping on his jeans, he went out into the living room and returned, carrying his case. He walked into the bathroom, and in seconds she heard the shower going. She got out of bed and plucked a robe from her closet, quickly tying herself into it, her fingers shaking. She felt storm-tossed, as if her world had been turned upside down and shaken. She couldn't think. She could only feel—and what she felt was pain.

She went out and started the coffee, and when she finished, the bedroom door opened and he strode out, fully dressed in dark gray pants and a light gray silk sweater. His jaw was smooth, his hair combed. "Your turn," he said curtly. The words stung—because she remembered how he had said them to her last night—and they had meant something entirely different. . . .

She escaped into the bathroom and went through her morning routine. The shower hissed over her in a warm stream, but nothing seemed to help the cold wall of hurt locked around her heart.

Ten minutes later, dressed for school in a close-fitting cranberry waist jacket, a silky white blouse with a bow at the throat, and a tailored black wool skirt, she walked out to the kitchenette. "You haven't poured yourself a cup of coffee."

"You seem to be out of milk," he replied, his face a cool mask.

"Am I? I'm sorry."

"Sit down and have yours. I'll catch a cup later."

Later, when he was driving down the road. . . . She took

a cup from the shelf and filled it with coffee, thinking she must somehow find the fortitude to endure these last few moments.

He sat slumped in the chair, his eyes averted from her. He stared at a point across the room—and what his thoughts were, she couldn't guess. His face betrayed nothing. After a silent moment, his blue eyes swung back to her. "Can I give you a ride to school?"

She shook her head, thinking she couldn't bear to say good-bye to him on the school grounds because she might burst into ridiculous tears. "No. I'll drive my own car."

His mouth tightened, but he didn't protest.

She made a nervous movement and pulled back her sleeve to look at her watch. "I must go," she said, her voice husky.

"Yes, I suppose you must," he agreed in a low, flat tone. He examined her, his eyes taking in her slim figure and her hair tied back in the turquoise holder. "Go ahead. I'll lock the door when I go."

"Ty—I—"

"Just go, honey," he said coolly. "After all, you don't want to—prolong the agony, do you?"

The blood rushed to her face. "No," she retorted, anger propelling her up off the chair. "There's not much point in that, is there?"

She got her coat, forced her feet to carry her to the threshold—and walked out of the door.

Numb with shock, she drove to school. The day stretched ahead of her like a yawning chasm, but somehow she managed to walk into the faculty room and face the teachers gathered there for the ritual cup of coffee before the first class. Hunt looked up at her from the end of the table, Eve to his right. Max, a peculiar, half-sympathetic look on his face, greeted her, his eyes flickering down to the other end of the table where the morning paper was spread and Ben Harris, the gym teacher who rarely bothered, was bent over it, reading something with avid interest. Another teacher leaned over his shoulder to read the same page. Instantly she knew something was wrong.

Eve got up and came to her. In a low tone, she asked, "Are you all right? Your face looks—"

"I'm fine," Leigh said grimly, lying.

Eve gave a nervous laugh. "It was something of a shock to us to find out we have a celebrity in our midst."

"I'm—not a celebrity."

"The morning paper says you are." Leigh felt the nerves in her stomach tighten. Her protest was automatic. "Really, I—"

Eve's cheeks colored. "It makes no difference to me who your parents were. And actually"—she hesitated—"I've become rather—fond of celebrities." She gave Leigh another bright, nervous smile and said in a rush, "I'm flying out to California this weekend. Deke wants me to come and be with him even if it's only for two days." The color climbed higher in her face. "I—couldn't say no."

"Eve, how wonderful." She forgot her own pain, forgot everything except that Eve deserved another chance at happiness, and Deke was interesting, intelligent, and seemed exactly right for Eve.

"What about you?" Eve whispered. "What's happening with tall, dark, and devastating?"

She steeled herself to say the words. "I—it's over."

Eve's face sobered. "Oh, darling, I'm so sorry. And here I am, hitting you with my good news."

"It's all right. You deserve your happiness. Take it while you can."

Max rose and came to her. His voice low, he said, "Better brace yourself. There's an article in the paper that pretty much tells everything about you and your parents. It's caused some—interesting reactions."

Reeling from this second shock, she went to stand behind Ben. There in secondary headlines in the "People in Art" section were the words, "Ty Rundell Rumored Interviewing Claire Foster's Daughter for New Book."

The article below gave a capsule description of her mother's career, her father's tragic death, and told of Leigh's career as a teacher.

For an instant she reeled with pain. Had Ty . . . a blinding blaze of truth washed over her. No, Ty would never do this to her. Only one man was responsible for this article, a man who wouldn't hesitate to use her name and destroy her anonymity to further his own ends. Paul. Paul had nearly destroyed her once, and he would have no qualms about doing it again if he stood to gain from it, though how he would, she couldn't guess. Ty had held her hand and comforted her that night in the city and made tender, passionate love to her last night, and he would never hurt her this way, he just wouldn't. In fact, if Ty had known about the article, she was sure he would have done everything in his power to stop it.

He wasn't like Paul. He wasn't anything like Paul. Shock sent nervous chills through her. A moment ago she hadn't known how much she trusted him. She would trust him with her life—for the rest of her life.

She whirled to Hunt. "Call Betty in to teach for me. I've got to go home."

He half rose out of his chair, his face concerned. "Are you ill?"

"No. Yes. I don't know. Here." She threw down her burden of papers, and they skittered across the top of the table, fanning out in front of Hunt like a deck of cards. "My plans are in there, along with the tests that have to be passed back to the kids. I'll talk to you later."

She flew out to the car and jerked open the door. The keys wouldn't go in the ignition because she was in a hurry, but after what seemed like an endless age, she got the car started. She drove around the circle and sped back down the hill toward Viola's house. If she could only catch him. . . .

The apartment door was unlocked. Her heart leaping with hope, she yanked the door open—only to find an empty, quiet apartment. He was gone. He had left the door open and the coffee server on, but he was gone.

Wild with fury—whether at herself for letting him go or at him for leaving, she wasn't sure which—she ran to the counter and switched off the warmer. In a frenzy she ran into the bedroom to throw things into a suitcase. She had a far better chance of catching him on the road if she left at once.

Knowing she probably had forgotten half a dozen things, and that it didn't matter in the slightest, she snapped her suitcase closed and snatched it up. At the door she fumbled with the self-locking button, her heart pounding—when she heard the familiar creak of the second riser. She jerked the door open wide—and saw him. He wore the leather oxblood jacket, and in his hand he carried a quart container of milk.

He reached the top of the stairs and turned toward her. Fear and excitement chased through her veins, and in her nervous state she said the first thing that came to her mind. "What are you doing here?"

"Getting some milk for my coffee," he said, as if it were the most natural thing in the world. "What are you doing here?" His eyes fell to the suitcase she held in her hand.

"I—" Faced with the warm-blooded reality of him, her courage drained away. "I remembered something I needed."

Slowly, he came down the hall toward her. "Me?" he sked softly.

She met his gaze steadily. "Yes."

In the soft light of the hall, his eyes seemed to burn over her. "Unlock the door."

She forced her hands to steadiness and did as he asked.

He picked up her suitcase and followed her inside, kicking the door shut behind him. He dropped her case to the floor, set the milk on the table, and turned. She stood in the middle of the room in a fog of uncertainty.

"What took you so long," he said silkily—and then he smiled. It was the most beautiful, self-assured, utterly arrogant male smile she had ever seen.

She threw herself into his arms, loving the rock-hard feel of his body braced against hers. "I didn't know how you felt."

"Liar," he breathed, smoothing her hair, his fingers finding and unclasping the turquoise holder and tossing it to the counter. Her hair tumbled free, and he threaded his fingers through it as if he were savoring its lush silkiness. "You must have known how I felt."

"I didn't—" Her arms tightened.

He leaned back against the counter, taking the full weight of her on his lean body, his warm mouth nuzzling her hair. "Why aren't you at school?"

"I came home because I saw this article and I knew Paul had talked about me and I knew you wouldn't and I—knew I loved you and there was no comparison between the two of you and I was crazy to think you would ever be like him—"

He clamped hard fingers around her upper arms and held her away to look into her face. "What did you say?"

"There was an article in the paper—"

"Not that. The part about loving me."

She flushed and slid her hands up the front of his chest under his jacket. "I didn't want to," she whispered. "I tried so hard not to fall in love with you—"

He caught her to him and planted a hard, possessive kiss on her lips. "But you did anyway," he said, with that self-satisfied look lifting the corners of his mouth, "just the way I fell in love with you. Oh God, honey, I love you so much. I can't believe you came back to me."

His mouth rained kisses over her face in a punishing reward. When he raised his head, she said in a throaty voice, "I'll give up my job," her heart kicking with joy, her fingers coming up to trace the generous curve of his mouth.

"No, not yet. I'll stay here and write—at least for the rest of the winter."

She held herself away from him. "You can't stop making films; you've got to go on doing what you're doing. I would never want that."

He gazed at her thoughtfully. "You have been doing some thinking, haven't you?"

"Maybe for the first time in my life I'm really thinking clearly. Thinking about what I want, what's possible for me—instead of who my mother was, or what happened to me because of her."

His smile blazed over her. "And to think I almost didn't let you walk out of that door this morning. Believe me, it took more courage and self-control to do that than it did to walk close to the edge of that rim yesterday afternoon." He locked his arms around her. "I kept thinking if you really cared about me, you wouldn't let me go—"

"And I kept thinking if you really cared about me, you wouldn't go—"

He unbuttoned her coat and let it slide to the floor. "Where were you going with the suitcase?"

"Out looking for you," she murmured, "to the end of the earth if I had to."

"Or even to Hollywood?" He tugged at the silk bow, his fingers loosening it. "I wanted to do this this morning when you walked out of that bedroom looking so prim and proper and ready for school—"

183

"Yes, even to Hollywood. And I wanted to do this," she said, reaching up and ruffling his hair, "when you walked out of the bedroom looking like the leading man in a cast of thousands."

"There's only one leading man I want to play," he muttered. "The role of husband and father. I won't settle for anything less than a lifetime run."

Her body sang with relief and joy. "Oh, Ty—" She gave him a brilliant smile.

"Do you have to go back to school?" he breathed, his voice husky as his fingers moved over her buttons. "If you do, you'd better go soon before I take you in the bedroom."

"I told Hunt to find a substitute. I have the day off."

"A whole day," he said, scooping her up into his arms. "Maybe we'll think of a way to spend it."

"You're the creative genius—any ideas?" She nestled in his arms, sweetly innocent.

He swung her to the bed and followed her down, his lips curved in a smile. "Oh, I'm sure I'll think of something—if the setting is right."

"What about the main characters? Do they know their lines?"

"They can improvise."

"They might get stuck on one idea—like—Ty Rundell, I love you, love you, love you." She reached up and clasped him around the neck, pulling him down to her.

He shrugged, his hands pulling her blouse away from her satiny skin. "Some lines bear repeating."

"I'll say it until you get tired of hearing it."

"You couldn't live that long, Leigh. Now stop talking and kiss me."

His warm mouth took hers with a possession that was echoed in the hungry claiming of her own. He was hers, and she was his, and they would have more than a night, they would have a lifetime of love to look back upon. She relaxed and clasped his nape to hold him close and let the sweet tide of passion sweep over her that only Ty's kiss could bring.

LOOK FOR NEXT MONTH'S
CANDLELIGHT ECSTASY ROMANCES ®

186 GEMSTONE, *Bonnie Drake*
187 A TIME TO LOVE, *Jackie Black*
188 WINDSONG, *Jo Calloway*
189 LOVE'S MADNESS, *Sheila Paulos*
190 DESTINY'S TOUCH, *Dorothy Ann Bernard*
191 NO OTHER LOVE, *Alyssa Morgan*
192 THE DEDICATED MAN, *Lass Small*
193 MEMORY AND DESIRE, *Eileen Bryan*

NEW DELL

Candlelight Ecstasy Supreme

TEMPESTUOUS EDEN,
by Heather Graham.
$2.50

Blair Morgan—daughter of a powerful man, widow of a famous senator—sacrifices a world of wealth to work among the needy in the Central American jungle and meets Craig Taylor, a man she can deny nothing.

EMERALD FIRE,
by Barbara Andrews
$2.50

She was stranded on a deserted island with a handsome millionaire—what more could Kelly want? Love.

NEW DELL

Candlelight Ecstasy Supreme

LOVERS AND PRETENDERS,
by Prudence Martin
$2.50

Christine and Paul—looking for new lives on a cross-country jaunt, were bound by lies and a passion that grew more dangerously honest with each passing day. Would the truth destroy their love?

WARMED BY THE FIRE,
by Donna Kimel Vitek
$2.50

When malicious gossip forces Juliet to switch jobs from one television network to another, she swears an office romance will never threaten her career again—until she meets superstar anchorman Marc Tyner.

When You Want A Little More Than Romance—

Try A Candlelight Ecstasy!

Dell **Wherever paperback books are sold!**

THE SEEDS OF SINGING
by Kay McGrath

To the primitive tribes of New Guinea, the seeds of singing are the essence of courage. To Michael Stanford and Catherine Morgan, two young explorers on a lost expedition, they symbolize a passion that defies war, separation, and time itself. In the unmapped highlands beyond the jungle, in a world untouched since the dawn of time, Michael and Catherine discover a passion men and women everywhere only dream about, a love that will outlast everything.

A DELL BOOK   19120-3 $3.95

At your local bookstore or use this handy coupon for ordering:

Dell

DELL BOOKS   THE SEEDS OF SINGING   19120-3 $3.95
P.O. BOX 1000, PINE BROOK, N.J. 07058-1000

Please send me the above title. I am enclosing $_____ (please add 75c per copy to cover postage and handling). Send check or money order—no cash or C.O.D.'s. Please allow up to 8 weeks for shipment.

Name _____

Address _____

City _____ State/Zip _____

Desert Hostage

Diane Dunaway

Behind her is England and her first innocent encounter with love. Before her is a mysterious land of forbidding majesty. Kidnapped, swept across the deserts of Araby, Juliette Barclay sees her past vanish in the endless, shifting sands. Desperate and defiant, she seeks escape only to find harrowing danger, to discover her one hope in the arms of her captor, the Shiek of El Abadan. Fearless and proud, he alone can tame her. She alone can possess his soul. Between them lies the secret that will bind her to him forever, a woman possessed, a slave of love.

A DELL BOOK 11963-4 $3.95

At your local bookstore or use this handy coupon for ordering:

| Dell | DELL BOOKS
P.O. BOX 1000, PINE BROOK, N.J. 07058-1000 | DESERT HOSTAGE 11963-4 $3.95 |

Please send me the above title. I am enclosing $_____ (please add 75c per copy to cover postage and handling). Send check or money order—no cash or C.O.D.'s. Please allow up to 8 weeks for shipment.

Name _____

Address _____

City _____ State/Zip _____

Seize The Dawn
by Vanessa Royall

For as long as she could remember, Elizabeth Rolfson knew that her destiny lay in America. She arrived in Chicago in 1885, the stunning heiress to a vast empire. As men of daring pressed westward, vying for the land, Elizabeth was swept into the savage struggle. Driven to learn the secret of her past, to find the one man who could still the restlessness of her heart, she would stand alone against the mighty to claim her proud birthright and grasp a dream of undying love.

A DELL BOOK   17788-X $3.50

At your local bookstore or use this handy coupon for ordering:

Dell	**DELL BOOKS** SEIZE THE DAWN 17788-X $3.50 P.O. BOX 1000, PINE BROOK, N.J. 07058-1000

Please send me the above title. I am enclosing $ _____ (please add 75c per copy to cover postage and handling). Send check or money order—no cash or C.O.D.'s. Please allow up to 8 weeks for shipment.

Mr./Mrs./Miss _____

Address _____

City _____ State/Zip _____